The Quest

Robert S Bucci

Copyright © 2014 Robert S Bucci

All rights reserved.
This novel is a work of fiction. Names, characters, places and incidents are either the product of the author's imagination, or, if real, used fictitiously. Any resemblance to any person or persons, living or dead, events or locales is entirely coincidental.

No part of this work may be reproduced, transmitted, stored, or used in any form or by any means graphic, electronic, or mechanical without the written consent of the author.

ISBN-10:1500970247
ISBN-13:978-1500970246

DEDICATION

For Ryan and Rebecca

Chapter One

Many centuries ago, when magic hung in the air and giants walked the earth, there lived a beautiful princess. No ordinary princess, this princess was special even among princesses, for beyond being merely beautiful, she was also kind and generous. The Princess lived in a magical time, a time when the world was new and people believed in dreams and wishes—or at least some people believed. Even though the world was young and mystifying, princes and princesses still fell in love and many a princess kept a watchful eye on distant hills hoping to catch a glimpse of her prince. And, many a prince searched and searched, hoping to find his princess over the crest of the next hill. Yet, of all the princes and princesses that ever lived, two very special people nearly did not find each other, for they lived on opposite sides of the world.

On the Princess's side of the world, the young Princess was beginning to lose all hope of finding her prince, fearing that her Queen Mother would never allow her to marry any prince, even if he were the kindest, noblest, or the most loving of all the world's princes. No princess ever loved her mother more, but the Princess could speak no words to move her mother's heart to let her marry, and the Princess was beginning to lose all hope.

There was, however, one person who offered the Princess hope and that was the Guard Captain, the person closest to being the father she had only met as a newborn infant, but had never known. Always there when the Princess needed someone to help her better understand her world and mother, the Captain would tell the Princess that it was not a cold heart that made her mother the way she was, but fear. Fear of losing her daughter. Sometimes crying and always pleading, the Princess would ask the Guard Captain, "Tell me, tell me, why does she not want me to marry?"

Yet, no matter how many times she asked, the Captain's answer was always the same, "Your mother loves you. When you are older, you will learn why she fears your marriage."

Confused and unable to understand why her mother would not allow her to marry, the Princess would plead for her to explain, but her only answer was, "When the time was right." At first, when the Princess was young, her requests had the pleadings of a child, but as she grew older and her questions more adult, it became more and more difficult for the Queen to simply say, "No."

As the years passed, the yearning of a young woman seeking to make her own life and happiness began to weigh heavily on the Queen's heart, for she loved her daughter dearly. But it was not the Princess's requests that touched her mother's heart, but her silence. The Princess began to realize that her mother concealed a deep secret that she would

and knew that she was entitled to all the life had to offer a young life

The Quest

not share, and it was that secret, that [could not share?] [which] prevented her mother from speaking the truth. The Princess had grown to learn that all too often, one might be called upon to sacrifice one's own happiness for those she served and loved—such was the life of a princess and daughter, or a queen and mother.

Yet, her mother had not been unmoved by her daughter's many requests to marry, and while they were no longer spoken, her mother could still hear them echoing in the [AMIDST] castle's rooms. A soft whisper, which made the Queen remember her own youth, and love for her dead husband the King. Yet, remembering the happiness was also tied to remembering the pain of her youth, linking the death and loss of her husband—with the fear of losing her daughter. It was those two feelings—joy and terror—that brought her to a plan that might allow her daughter to marry. Hopefully, it would also keep her daughter safe.

Early one morning, after a restless night planning and thinking, the Queen asked the Princess to come to her room. There, among her many memories, the Queen told the Princess of her plan. Any man able to fulfill three challenges of her choosing would be allowed to ask her daughter to marry. While the Princess looked upon her mother with thankfulness and a new found hopefulness, she was also able to see a glimpse of deep fear that she had never seen before in her mother's eyes. When the Princess asked what caused such pain [TROUBLED HER], the Queen only looked lovingly at the Princess and taking her hand, called for the Guard Captain. Upon his immediate and silent arrival, she told him of her

→ as she grew older

plan, and commanded him to issue a "Royal Challenge" and to proclaim it throughout the land.

As the months slipped away, the proclamation did little to raise the Princess's hope, since the "Royal Challenge" brought failure to all those attempting the challenge. With every failure and passing season, each new day became more difficult for the young Princess. Life also became more difficult for the Queen Mother. Each new challenger found the Queen becoming more and more guarded of her daughter, as if each new suitor for the Princess's hand brought her closer and closer to danger.

So fearful was the Queen for her daughter's safety, that she rarely allowed her to venture anywhere alone. Nevertheless, the young Princess, from the moment she learned to walk, had learned to slip away from the watchful eye of the Queen Mother and sneak off to her secret room high amidst the clouds in the castle tower. If the Princess's room was secret, it was only secret to the Queen, since it had been set aside by the Guard Captain, as a playroom for the young Princess. All the castle guards knew of it, as well as the villagers who would often spy her standing by the window. Yet, no one spoke of it, no one pointed, and no one ever called out to her. The room was the villagers' secret as much as it was the Princess's.

The Queen's Royal Guard, while faithful to her every need and request, would let the Princess sneak off to her room. The guards suffered much abuse for their kindness, for the Queen, fearful for her daughter's safety, would call them lazy and idle

The Quest

when the Princess was nowhere to be found. Yet, all the guards loved the Princess, so they gladly suffered the Queen's insults since they knew that even a young Princess needed a special place to be just a young girl.

Nestled high above the village in her secret room, her generous and kind nature flourished. Always wishing to be helpful, villagers would say that she reached the side of an injured child before the first cry was heard, even by the child's mother. Farmers struggling with a cart of goods would turn to find her collecting whatever might have been bounced to the ground, and all the children said that she was the best storyteller in the village. Among the elders of the village, it was said that she was just like her mother the Queen, but the younger villagers could never understand why it was true. Everyone believed her mother to be an honest, fair, and generous queen, whom they loved dearly, but one who never seemed to be able to return the love given her.

As often as she could wander off, unseen by the Queen, she would hurry to her room. Where, as the Princess grew older, she would search the horizon by day seeking the prince who might answer the challenge, and by night, search for a new star—one she had not already wished upon. After years of wishing, she could no longer find a star she hadn't already wished upon, and would instead search the heavens for a falling star, knowing that if she wished upon it, her wish was sure to come true.

One evening, as her tired eyes begged for sleep, she struggled to remain awake just a little longer. Standing by the room's largest window, she forced herself to stay awake while she peered into the midnight sky. Finally, too tired to remain awake any longer, she sleepily crisscrossed the room to lie upon her small daybed tucked away beneath a tiny, oval window that opened to the heavens above. Just as she was about to drift off to sleep, she took one last glance out the tiny window and saw what she had long been searching for, a falling star.

Knowing exactly what to wish, because she had memorized her simple wish when just a child, she snuggled beneath the tiniest of her wishing windows and wrapping herself in her favorite quilt, whispered, "May my prince safely find his way to me." So tired and happy was the young Princess that she was almost asleep before the final word slipped past her lips.

She slept throughout the night, and was woken by the early sun pouring its light and warmth upon her face. She lay motionless and tightly snuggled within her blankets and quilts until she was sure that she had not merely dreamed of the falling star. She sprang from her bed filled with joy and hope. So happy was the Princess, that for the first time ever, she was not troubled by her mother's scolding for not being in her room in the early morning.

What the Princess did not know was that at the very moment she made her wish, far away—so far that it was exactly on the opposite side of the world, a young Prince filled with new found hope was waving his final goodbye to the people of his village.

The Quest

***

And so it was, princesses waited, and princes searched to find their perfect love. Yet, in one faraway village, there was a prince who almost gave up hope of finding a princess to share his life. His village was so distant from the rest of the world, that he could walk for days and days and never reach another village. Each and every time he set out on a journey to find the princess that appeared often in his dreams, his village would celebrate his quest with a loud and happy feast—hopeful that this time he would return with his bride. Instead, they found themselves greeting the same weary Prince returning home, alone and sad. Each time, upon his gloomy return, the town folks would wait at the village gate to offer the disappointed Prince a cooling drink of well water and a pat on the back, while offering words of encouragement, "maybe next time, maybe next time." Words that the Prince had heard so many times before; they made him cringe with despair and gloom.

No prince could have been loved more by his people. Since his father the King's mysterious death while standing guard outside the village gate, on a the night when the stars blinked, and later his mother's death from a broken heart, all the villagers felt as if they had a hand in raising him.

Orphaned and alone at a young age, some would say that the villagers helped and looked out for him as would a parent. In his heart, the Prince called them family. Like his father the King and later his mother the Queen, the Prince would only accept half the tribute brought to him each year by the villagers, and half of that he would set aside for when the harvest was less than his people needed to survive. It was because of his love and generosity and that of his parents before him, that the village and its people prospered in good as well as bad times. It was a wonderful place to live. Yet amidst all the happiness something was missing, something that the villagers would do anything to find.

As the seasons passed and the Prince no longer journeyed each spring in search of a princess bride, the villagers came to fear that he had given up all hope. Although the Prince was still as kind and good as ever, the villagers saw sadness in his eyes that the Prince could not mask behind a smiling face or hide behind his long hair. This was too much to bear for the villagers and the town square was always abuzz with, "We have to do something,"

"He's a good man—we need to find him a bride."

"Something has to be done—we must do something."

Taking up the challenge, the town folks began to meet in secret each night since they knew that the Prince would object, for he would tell them that they should be home caring for their own families. When the town was supposed to be sleeping, men and woman, as well as all the girls and boys of the village, would discuss what needed to be done. However, not knowing any princesses, or even knowing which path would lead to the door of a fair and beautiful one, they, too, soon began to give up hope.

One evening, as the room fell quieter and quieter, and hope was draining away, a small voice was heard. "Well, if we can't find a princess, maybe a princess can find us." At first, the thought of such a thing only brought laughter from the children, groans from the men, and hmmmms from the woman, but then the voice was heard again, "Maybe if we let the world know that we welcome travelers, a traveler will know of such a princess."

It took a while for the idea to sink in, but since it was such a good idea, it did not take all that much time. Quickly, it was decided the little village would do all that it could to become known as the best place to rest for a tired traveler. They would roll out the welcome mat.

There was, however, one little problem. If no one ever came to the village now, how would anyone know that their village was a good place to visit and rest? Ideas abounded, most were discussed and all were dismissed. On and on they talked, and finally as the morning sun began to peek over the distant hills in the east, it was agreed that every day they would send one of the village's faster runners, who after running for several hours, would stick a sign into the ground saying "Visitors Welcomed—this way →."

At the end of one week, they had placed seven signs. After three more weeks, they had put up twenty-nine signs, since someone took two signs by mistake and put both of them in the same place. Now, all they had to do was wait.

Chapter Two

They did not have to wait very long. Soon guests began to constantly stop by the village, sometimes for a quick meal, sometimes for a chat with the friendly villagers, and sometimes to spend the night. Travelers told other travelers, who told other travelers, and before too long, the tiny village became the crossroads of the world. Although all were welcomed and travelers soon came to say that no village anywhere in the world was a better place to rest or was kinder to visitors, all were required to answer the same question—"Do you know which princess is the most beautiful and kind in all the world?" Sadly, no one could say that they had ever met such a rare and special princess.

One day, a slow-walking man, with eyes that told he had seen much of the world, asked a kindly woman, "Could you please spare a bit of simple fare for a weary wanderer?"

Since guests were always welcomed in the village he was quickly offered a place at her table for supper. Watching him from across the table, as he ate slowly to savor every morsel, the kindly woman excused herself and ran to fetch her two neighbors to join her and the slow-walking man for after-dinner-sweets. It was not long before the two neighbors shared the kindly woman's excitement and belief that he might be the one who could help them. They talked more than the he did, but they stopped to listen carefully each time he did speak. His hosts waited long into their conversation, since he looked so tired and famished, before asking, "Do you know which princess is the most beautiful and kindest?"

He sat perfectly still for a long time thinking, with only the gentle swaying of his pipe to reveal that he was still awake. At last, he spoke, "Mostly all princesses are beautiful—that's one of the things that make them princesses, but I have come across one princess that also has a beautiful heart, which is a far rarer gift than a mere pretty face."

Although the slow-walking man had told only three villagers, and one of the three was known to be quite hard of hearing, it was not long before the entire kingdom was buzzing with the news. By the time dusk had begun to fall upon the land, and the farmers had returned from their farms and pastures, a large crowd had gathered near the Prince's small, but neat, castle. Never one to refuse guests, he opened the castle doors to his friends. Quickly the small castle was overflowing and no one could move without bumping into someone or stepping on someone else's toes. It was so crowded that the children had to be hoisted to the rafters, where they watched and listened not making a sound, lest they remind their parents that they should be home asleep in their beds.

All the adults began talking at once, and while the Prince could make no sense of what was being said, he could easily tell they were excited about something. Finally, he hopped atop the tallest table and asked for quiet. Keeping with the custom of the time, a hush settled upon the room. The quiet did not last long, for when he asked what news they brought, everyone started talking yet again.

Once more, the Prince asked for quiet and called out to the quiet Blacksmith who always had time to listen to the chatter of a young boy—or a young and talkative Prince, "What brings you merry villagers to my home?"

"We have found her, sire," the Blacksmith replied.

"Found whom?" the Prince asked.

"Sire, it may be best if we speak in private—like we often did in my smithy." So, off they went, the Prince wearing the fine coat that the villagers had given him on his birthday, and the Smithy dressed in a black leather apron that matched his hands, blackened, by many years of working fire and iron. Walking together, everyone could easily see the deep affection they held for each other, one that had been forged over a hot fire and many years of long friendship. Everyone watched and strained to hear what the two friends tucked away in the distant corner were saying, but as hard as they tried to listen, even with their ears turned in that direction, not a word could be heard.

Finally, after several minutes that seemed to take forever to the villagers, the Prince once again

The Quest

climbed atop the banquet table. More silent moments passed with the Prince quietly looking upon everyone's face. Gazing into their hopeful eyes, he spoke to the waiting villagers. "Dear friends, even after years of knowing that you have always honored me with your kindness, I never truly realized just how kind and giving you are. Your thoughtfulness has touched my heart." Then, in a louder and even happier voice, "As I set out on the quest you have brought me, know this, even if I fail to find the kind and beautiful princess I seek, I shall return a happy man, for you have blessed me with your kindness."

Slowly at first, and then moving faster and faster, a smile spread from face-to-face, until the room was aglow with a single smile, and when it had reached the face of even the smallest child, a roar was heard—"hip, hip, hooray." So loud was their chant, the children were rattled from the rafters where they sat.

In the days that followed, much work had to be done. The slow-walking man was brought to the castle, and although the road leading back to the Princess's castle had grown hazy in his mind—he told the Prince and the mapmakers to follow the sun in the morning and keep the afternoon sun to his back. Knowing the dangers the Prince would face and fearful the villagers would become angry with him for setting the Prince upon such a perilous trek, he secretly told the Prince that the journey would be one filled with danger, peril, and many challenges, and the passage would not be easy, even for a man of the Prince's strength and youth. After spending as much time with the Prince as the slow-walking man could offer, he bid his farewell, and began to set upon his own delayed journey. As he was about to leave the castle, he slowly turned and, straightening up, he raised his head even higher, and whispered in the Prince's ear. Several town folks standing nearby thought that he spoke a final goodbye, while others noticed that the Prince's hand reached for a nearby chair, as if to steady himself.

While the Prince and the slow-walking man had been discussing the journey, the rest of the village was hard at work preparing what they could to ease the hardship of such a demanding journey. The town's cobbler busied himself making a pair of comfortable walking shoes for the Prince, while the tailor stitched and snipped and snipped and stitched—finally creating a suit of clothes that would befit a prince in rain or sunshine. The baker mixed and kneaded and baked, until he had created a fine cake that he cut into little squares and wrapped in large fig leaves. Carefully wrapped, he told the Prince that they would remain fresh for weeks and he would never hunger.

"They're delicious, too," the Prince added after tasting the baker's creation.

When the clothes and shoes had been fitted, the food packed, and the maps drawn, a village banquet was held to celebrate everyone's new found hope. Beginning early one morning, the celebration was over well before sunset ended the day, since everyone wanted the Prince to be well rested to begin his journey early the following day. The night passed quickly, and early the next morning, even

The Quest

before the sun had risen, the Prince rose from bed and dressed in the clothes and shoes that the tailor and cobbler had made for him. Once dressed, he walked slowly through his beloved family home, putting everything in order. Once accomplished [Completed], he shuttered the castle's windows lest it rain while he was away. Leaving his home, he slowly walked to the village gate, trying to capture one final look at the village's great beauty. With not another soul to be seen, he was pleased that the town folks, having had such a joyful time the night before, were still peacefully sleeping in their beds.

Hoping to slip quietly out the village gate and not wanting to wake the villagers, he carefully slid the latch open, so as not to make a sound, which might wake the roosters, which in turn might wake the village. Once he had opened the gate, he slipped backwards through it, trying to memorize the smallest detail of the place he loved best and knew he would miss dearly.

Only after shutting the gate and clinking the latch tight, did he turn to begin his journey. When he did, he turned to find the entire village, standing shoulder-to-shoulder, lining both sides of the path. Starting with the youngest and ending with the oldest, the entire village waited to wish him well. Boys bowed, young girls curtsied, and men patted him on the back with one hand as they shook his hand with the other. Mothers kissed him and all the grandmothers pinched his cheeks. Finally, as he neared the end of well-wishers, he saw his friend the Smithy. Silently they stood, no words were necessary and none passed over their [were spoken] lips; they only needed to look at each other for their eyes said all that they needed to say.

By now, the sun was already high in the sky, and as the Prince walked further and further into the unknown, he did so with great courage and hope because he knew that he was indeed fortunate to have such good and noble friends. As he was about to cross over a distant hill, that would soon hide his village, he turned to take one final look. Although he could not truly see his friends, he knew they were waving, and he waved a long goodbye himself. It was at that moment, on the other side of the darkened world, that a young Princess, wishing upon a falling star, bonded their lives together.

Chapter Three

The journey, while full of hope and anticipation, was nevertheless a difficult one. Days first, and then weeks of travel passed, and the Prince's village slipped further and further away. The brooks and rich green grass that were present at the beginning of his trek, were now replaced by a scorched brown earth. Although the journey was difficult, never once did he give up hope. Onward the Prince trudged, facing the sun each morning and walking away from the sun once it began to slip back to earth.

With each new day of his journey, the warning the slow-walking man had shared with him and him alone echoed in his ears, "Be weary at all times, and when the earth trembles—hide yourself; when the earth opens near your feet—run." Even more troubling was what else the slow-walking man had told him, the only warning that seemed real to the Prince, "The Queen's challenges will be difficult before you can ask for the hand of the Princess in marriage."

What did it all mean? What might make the world tremble or the earth open beneath his feet?

And what challenges must be answered before he would be allowed to ask for the Princess's hand? On and on he walked, his mind racing faster than his feet. "What does it all mean? What does it mean, hide when the earth trembles, run when the earth opens at your feet? What would cause the earth to tremble or the ground to open? What could the challenges require? Will I be able to answer the challenges? WHAT does it mean?" As the burning sun beat down upon him, nothing made sense anymore and the Prince was only sure that the slow-walking man had told less than he knew.

Yet, no matter how weary he grew, never did the Prince think about returning to the safety of his village. He was determined to find his way to the Princess, even if danger followed danger every step of the way.

One day, while searching the horizon for the spires of the Princess's castle and exhausted from the day's journey, he happened to gaze upon a forest far off in the distance. No ordinary forest, the Prince could see that even from far away, the trees of this forest were the largest he had ever seen anywhere in his travels. *At last, shade from the burning sun and hopefully water, too, maybe even something to eat*. Off he went, walking and running, never resting, moving faster than he had ever walked or ran since his journey's start.

After many tiring hours of difficult travel, he found himself standing among the trees, trees so tall that their green leaves lay hidden among the clouds. Weary from his walk, too tired to explore, all he longed for was rest and sleep. Spying a golden

The Quest

haystack set beside a large hill, he only had strength enough to trudge up the hill, where he collapsed upon the haystack, falling into a deep slumber.

He was suddenly snapped awake by a terrible shaking. Unsure whether he had slept briefly or for a very long time, all he knew was that the earth was trembling and the wind howling. Not knowing what to do, but remembering the words of the slow-walking man, he clutched tight the haystack, realizing for the first time that it was like no other hay he had ever known before. This hay was softer than the hay that grew in his village, and hay never moved, at least not any that he had ever known. Holding on for life and fearing that he would never complete his journey, he found himself lifted higher and higher, nearly as high as the trees touching the clouds. Amazed at what was happening, yet too brave to be afraid, all he could do was gaze upon a world the likes of which he had never seen before. Scanning the horizon, and forgetting the danger before him, he heard himself shout, "There, there is the Kingdom I seek."

"Hoooo! Am I so lonely, that I am now hearing voices?" bellowed a voice so deep and loud that it made the Prince quiver and nearly lose his grip.

His ears ringing, the best the Prince could do was yell himself, "There is no need to shout. I can hear you, but where are you my loud friend?"

"Where am I? Where are you friend, if truly a friend?" came a voice from nowhere. "Many say they are friend, but few are friend indeed. Now, tell me, where are you hiding?"

Still grasping tight the haystack, the Prince brushed himself off, and standing as tall as he could with nowhere to place his feet, spoke in a calm, yet loud voice. "Friend, Princes do not hide, I am standing in a haystack which has taken flight—with me in it," replied the Prince.

"What haystack? There is no haystack. Do not try to fool me, you would be wise to be truthful" bellowed the unknown speaker.

"Princes do not lie; I shall climb to the top of the haystack to aid your poor eyesight." Climb is what the Prince did, and after much effort, he soon found himself staring at the largest lips he had seen or could have imagined. Nearly out of breath from the difficult climb, the Prince shouted, "Friend, can you feel this?" as he quickly yanked a strand of hay.

A loud yelp swiftly followed the yank, followed by a quieter voice pleading, "Sorcerer, I beg you, do not cast a spell on me."

Laughing loudly, the Prince proclaimed, "I am no sorcerer, I am merely a prince and a small prince at that, and all I did was pull one of your whiskers. Carefully now, very carefully, lift your hand under your beard, and I will hop onto it."

Doing as the Prince asked, the giant stared in bewilderment at the Prince, who having popped out of his beard, now stood in the palm of his hand. Watching the Prince laugh with great glee, stumbling all the while, it was not long before the giant too began laughing. The giant's laughing only made the Prince laugh harder, which only made the giant laugh harder and louder. Laughing until their sides hurt and no longer able to stand, each begged the other to stop laughing. Even amidst all the laughing, it was not long before each knew that they had made a wondrous new friend, and while the Prince had difficulty with his new friend's name, Brewster, he thought it a good and noble name, one that befit a giant.

As quickly as the rising yellow sun had begun that remarkable day, a sinking orange sun was swiftly bringing it to an end. Knowing that night would soon bring darkness, they labored to find fallen branches and kindling to build a fire. Working together, it was not long before they were resting before the warm glow of a campfire, the Prince thinking it was the largest fire he had ever seen and Brewster finding it difficult to keep warm before such a tiny tinkling of a blaze.

Lying beneath the stars and among the fire's dancing shadows, they made a most interesting sight. The Prince sitting high atop a tree stump where the giant had placed him, while the giant laid stretched out on his side. So large was the giant that even perched high above the ground near the giant's head, the darkened sky and the fading light of the flickering flames made it difficult for the Prince to see all the way to his new friend's feet.

Long through the night, and well after the once-blazing fire had faded to dim orange embers they continued to talk by the light of the moon and the stars. The Prince told of his quest to find the princess who was kind of heart. He told him about all that his village had done, and although he spoke freely about everything, he kept his fears and the slow-walking man's warnings to himself.

Brewster, also talked freely, telling the Prince stories of days long gone, days when the earth was young and giants were needed. Stories about when traveling from village to village, giants had been called upon to slay the many dragons that brought fear and terror. Now, with the dragons gone, and villagers no longer even remembering a time when dragons roamed the earth, giants had nothing left to do. No longer needed, the giants soon become sad and lonely and it wasn't long before they too, like the dragons, began to wander the land hiding from view only to slowly vanish from the earth, with no one to mourn their passing.

Hearing of his new friend's woe, and knowing that his own hope had been renewed by his quest, the Prince began to think that perhaps the giant would benefit from joining in his quest. Since it had brought him hope, maybe it would do the same for his new friend. Wishing to bring hope to his friend, but knowing hope can only be discovered by the person seeking its comfort and guidance, the Prince began telling of the difficult journey he was to continue in the morning. He talked of the great distance he needed to travel, how he doubted his legs could ever carry him on so great a journey, and his grief over not being able to reach the Princess.

Finally, although he knew in his heart that he would never really quit, he looked into Brewster's eyes and said, "I must accept my fate, I will never be able to reach the Princess's Kingdom, so maybe it is best that I return to my village. At least my journey has been one of great adventure and discovery, and I will be sure to tell them of the

The Quest

good and kindly giant I befriended. Well, best we try to get some sleep; I must begin my journey back home in the morning."

With more to say, but too tired to go on talking, the Prince and giant closed their eyes. The Prince, weary and tired from the day's excitement and long walk, quickly fell to sleep, while Brewster thought long into the night. Finally, after much tossing and turning by Brewster, the Prince was rustled from his sleep, just long enough to hear him murmur, "I know what I'll do." Once spoken, his words were swiftly followed by the swaying sound of the giant's breathing as he soundly slumbered through the night.

The following morning, it was well after sunrise when Brewster woke to find the Prince already packing his few belongings. "Well, I guess it's time for me to start my journey home. Although I return without a princess, I can still say that I have met a wonderful giant, a true friend."

"Not so fast! Do you wish to disappoint your villagers after all their planning and work? What kind of prince would do that?"

"Maybe you're right, maybe I could make the trip if I had some help, but even with all the help my friends have given me, the trip has proven to be far too long and difficult. Perhaps, if I knew a shorter way to the Princess's castle," said the Prince. After a moment of silence, with the Prince looking as if he was deep in thought, he continued, "Wait, maybe with your…No, I have no right to ask your help; but, together, we could make the journey quickly. No, you've got too much to do, but then, maybe, with your long legs, and me on your shoulder, I could make the trip far more quickly than I could if I were alone. No, that would be too much to ask of a great and noble giant."

Stopping the Prince before he could continue, Brewster rose up, and standing even taller than the Prince remembered, announced, "It might do my legs good to get a little exercise. We will start our journey when we are through packing, but first, we must eat."

Not too much time later, but before the sun was full yellow in the sky and while the Prince was repacking after his second breakfast and Brewster's first, the earth began to tremble yet again. At first, the Prince paid it no mind, but then seeing that Brewster was napping by what was left of the morning's fire, he hurried to where the giant slept and tugging at his ear, shouted, "Wake friend, get up, danger approaches."

Half-listening and half-sleeping Brewster groggily replied, "Fear not, my friend, danger is not at hand, it must be my brother Duncan, for he often wanders this forest." Turning back towards the rumbling earth and looking above the swirls of dust moving ever closer, the Prince noticed the large eyes first, partly because they were so big, but also because having met one giant, seeing another giant no longer seemed very strange. However, while the Prince may not have thought it strange to see another giant, it was difficult not to stare at Duncan's large eyes, for they were as large as the moon when it first appears over the horizon.

With each passing second and step that

The Quest

brought the giant closer and closer, the more the earth shook and his body trembled. The earth was quaking so much, that the Prince was shaken clear out of his shoes. Nearer and nearer the giant came and just as the Prince was getting used to the shaking, quaking, and trembling, he was startled anew as the two giants exchanged greetings.

"Hello, Brewster my brother, what new pet has found you now?"

"Welcome brother, but this is no pet, he is a prince, and a good prince at that."

"Still picking up strays I see."

"He is no stray, Brother Duncan. Shall I hold him closer so you can have a better look?"

"Always the jokester I see, you know well enough that I can see him perfectly, all the way to the hole in his left sock. Are you sure he is a prince?"

The Prince, not remembering whether there really was a hole in his sock, did wish he had tied his shoes tighter that morning. Trying not to look at his feet, for he was a Prince, it was still difficult not to sneak a peek. At least it was, until he realized that the two brothers where playing a joke on him.

Watching the two brothers embrace, it reminded him how much he missed the family that was taken from him much too soon. Yes, the villagers were his adopted family, but there was something special about family members that looked a little like you did, spoke the same way you did, liked the same foods, shared the same sorrows, and laughed at the same joys. It was just special. He missed his parents, and never understood why they were taken from him. One day his father was alive and well, the next morning he was gone. Some say that he traded his life for those of the villagers, but no one was ever sure. All he knew was that the villagers found him lying beside the main gate where he had fallen while standing guard beyond the safety of the village. All that was certain was that all the villagers said the stars blinked that evening, some believed it was sorrow that made them blink; others believed it was a great evil that passed overhead. The Prince, like his mother, believed that it was both sorrow and evil that made the stars blink. Trying to shake off the sorrow of remembering and wishing to give his two new friends time alone, he busied himself by studying his maps and taking stock of his dwindling supplies.

Not long later, Brewster approached the Prince and spoke, "My brother Duncan wishes to join us on our quest. What do you say, shall we have him?"

Smiling broadly, the Prince said, "I can think of no better companion to have on our journey. But before we go, do you think dear friend that with your strong eyes you can help thread this needle so that I can darn my sock."

Handing it to Duncan, the Prince laughed as Duncan's large hands struggled to thread the tiny needle, first moving it and then the thread back and forth. Unable to find the needle's almost invisible eye, Duncan never realized that now the joke was on him.

Chapter Four

Now that it had been agreed they would continue the journey together, it was well into midday before they were finished talking. Wishing to find themselves closer to their quest before the sun set, they made haste and set off on their journey. They traveled farther in one-half day than the Prince alone had traveled in three, all before the sun dipped beneath the earth's edge.

Sometimes the Prince would walk, and sometimes he rode high above the earth, alternating between the shoulders of the two giant brothers. Whether walking or riding, the Prince and his new friends talked about everything, the changing world, the plants and animals they had discovered, and the worlds that they had not known until they had met each other. Interestingly, as the days passed, the giants began to talk more about the future than they did the past.

Whereas, both talked about the early days when they vanquished the dragons and dark creatures that roamed the earth and ate the food and livestock of villagers when they first started their journey, now they began to talk about what new adventures their journey would bring tomorrow and the next day. Their mood began to change, change for the better. It would have been difficult for the Prince to think them happier than when they first met, but now they were funnier and even happier with each new day. With their new found happiness, the trip became more joyous with each step. Happily, they bounded along, each step lighter than the one before, and it wasn't long before first one, then two, and then three days were brought to an end by the setting sun.

It was only after setting up camp and building a fire after their third day of walking together, that they realized that they had walked further than any day before. Once dinner had been prepared and eaten, little time was spent talking that evening, for they had talked and walked the entire day away. Early into the evening, even before the fire turned to embers, all three were sleeping soundly. Although the two giants slept soundly that evening, the Prince's sleep was riddled with dreams about what was to come, which like many of the nights before, often found him waking more tired than when he had gone to sleep.

Although the Prince's dreams were vivid, it was the same each morning; he awoke unable to remember but tiny threads of his dreams—the death of his father and the warnings of the slow-walking man. Even when he did remember his dreams, there was always a feeling that there was some part of the dream he could not remember, something always just out of reach. Each morning it was the same, it was not what he remembered, but what he did not remember and could not understand that made his legs wobble and his body tingle.

On the fourth day of the their journey, the Prince knew that they did not have far to travel for even he could see, from atop Brewster's shoulders, the spiraling towers of the castle he hoped held the Princess and his happiness. While he and Brewster were winding their way between the trees and streams that now stood before them, Duncan would often stop and stand with his large eyes peering into the distance. Calling out to Duncan, the Prince asked, "Do we need fear what lies in the distance?"

Duncan turned, and smiling at the Prince, finally spoke, "Dear friend, it appears that you will get a chance to meet the last of the brothers three, for I see our younger brother Otis off in the distance."

After the two brothers gave a shout, and after the echo stopped ringing, a quiet voice was heard, "There really is no reason to shout, I heard your heavy footsteps long before you caught a glimpse of me, really both of you were never light on your feet."

Just when the Prince believed that having already met two giants, no new wonders could possibly exist, here was a giant with the largest ears that he had ever seen. Trying not to stare, all he could think was that they were large enough for him to stand in without bumping his head. Yet, as large as his ears were, he looked very much like his two brothers. Yes, they were different, but there was no denying them brothers. He knew that their hearts were the same, to say nothing of their smile.

It was impossible to see the three brothers together without knowing that they were joined by a deep affection for one another, an affection they had no difficulty sharing with others. The Prince could not imagine any situation where they would not stop to help someone needing their help, and it was then that he came to know just how lost they were when unable to be of help. Now, a band of four, they made camp for the evening and prepared a large supper to celebrate their reunion. Talking late into the night, it was a chance to relive the past several days with their newest companion. How the Prince first met Brewster, when Duncan later joined the quest and could not thread the needle, the long trek through the forest and plains, and how the Prince got a chance to fly in a haystack.

It did not take long before Otis decided that he too would join in the journey; all convinced that between the four of them, no challenge could defeat them. While none boasted about their own greatness, each heaped praise upon the others. That was just the way they were. Although they knew that together they possessed great strength and even great wisdom, all knew it was the Prince's search for love, and their deep friendship that would be the key to their success. Finally, after even the moon had vanished from the night sky, it was decided that rest was needed for the difficult journey that lay before them.

While sleep did not come easy to any of them, all remained quiet so as not to wake the others. No band of travelers could have been greater friends. Rising early the next morning, the Prince learned that rising early for the giants and rising early for him were quite different, for ~~when the~~ brothers woke, the Prince had already built a roaring fire and a breakfast of Griddlecakes were sizzling over the fire.

Waking from his sleep, Otis, the newest member of the group, announced, "Ah, it looks like our Prince is anxious to begin the journey, this Princess must be beautiful."

***

While the four travelers sat eating their breakfast and preparing to renew their journey, far away, the Princess spent her days lost in thought, thinking, or rather hoping that dreams do come true. Days first, and then weeks, had passed since she had glimpsed the falling star and made her wish, and while she still believed that dreams do come true, she did begin to wonder if her shooting star had been merely a dream. Each new morning found the Princess hurrying to her secret room to scan the horizon for sight of a Prince, and each evening found her lying in bed hoping that maybe tomorrow would bring her Prince.

Seeing the Princess each morning spring up the stairs to her lofty hideaway and slowing descending each night, the Guard Captain, ~~so as not to disturb the Princess~~, quietly stood watch ~~in the tower~~. One day, the Princess found him waiting for her as she winded her way down the spiral stairs.

"Princess, may I inquire as to why you have been so sad of late, especially these past few days?"

Looking into his eyes, as she had done many times before, she slowly realized how much his eyes had changed over the many years of her life, reflecting each passing year they had grown older. Yet, while his eyes had grown older, as had hers, she still saw him through the same eyes she had as a child. He was the man she had always sought when scared, when lonely, and when she needed a father. She had always known that she looked to him as a daughter would to a father, but now she realized just how much he meant to her.

"Captain, come sit beside me on the stairs. No, not that one, this one, for this is the step that you and I first sat upon before you showed me my secret room." Seeing a look of surprise in the Guard Captain's eyes, the Princess continued, "Did you think I forgot?"

"Princess, that was many years ago, you were a tiny child then, but how could you remember?"

"Friend and protector, there has never been a time I ascended these stairs without glancing upon that one step. I remember all; I remember the many stories you told me, while we sat upon that very step, about my father and your adventures together. It is through you that I have come to know my father. Mother rarely speaks of him, since doing so causes her such pain."

As always, it was impossible for the Princess to speak of her mother's pain without her head slowly sinking as she spoke, a pain that had now come to weigh heavily upon the Princess also.

As if to lift her burden onto himself, the

Guard Captain tenderly lifted the Princess's chin, and spoke, "Child, it too causes me pain to speak of him, it reminds me just how much he is missed. But, over the years, I have learned that speaking of him, especially to you, has helped keep him alive. Telling you of our adventures together, allows me to see him in you, your smile, your winning ways, your kindness, and most of all your hope and faith in the future. You keep him alive. He lives in you, and also through you."

They sat shoulder to shoulder for a long time, each silently remembering all the times that they had sat together on the stairs. The Captain thinking of the joy she brought to him while listening to her dream about the future or talking about her many pets or what she had learned that day. She sat thinking also, thinking about the father she had never known, and his friend that she had become acquainted with instead. She also knew why her father had befriended such a man and why he had made him Captain. He was a good man. Knowing this also made her know her father, because a man like the Captain would only be friend and brother to a good man. If the Captain called her father friend, her father must have been special to know such loyalty from a man as good as the Captain.

Yet, as much as she had learned from her guardian and protector, there was always a piece missing, a piece that only her mother could provide and she knew that this was a piece that her mother guarded tight and always kept well-hidden. It was no use asking the Captain; because it was the only question he would not answer, except to say, "When you are older, your mother will tell you."

Knowing what the Captain would never answer, the Princess turned to him and did ask, "Will I ever know happiness, even if only in the future?"

Smiling, the Guard Captain straight away replied, "You will, dear Princess, happiness cannot be kept from someone who brings so much happiness to others. That is your gift, one you have generously shared with others. Someday, although I am not sure when, the gifts you have given to others will be returned to you, with the love of those you love added to it." Then, realizing that this might be an answer understood by a man of his age and experience, but not by one so young, added, "Yes, happiness will come to you. Maybe, just maybe, it lies just beyond the morning's sunrise—so keep hope alive."

Then, after flashing a smile, one which the Princess had learned the meaning of long ago, spoke once more, "I have almost forgot, your mother worries where you are, I have told her that you were out among the villagers, but now you must hurry back before she sends out the guard for both of us." As always, the Captain rose first and offered his hand to the Princess. As she always did, she took his hand, but this time she refused to let go, and together, off they walked.

Later that evening, while wrapped within her quilt and snuggled in her bed, she thought of what the Guard Captain had said earlier that evening; maybe hope did lie just beyond the

The Quest

village's rim where the sun would rise the following morning. Holding tight ~~what the~~ Guard Captain had said earlier in the day, a peaceful sleep descended upon the young Princess. When the Princess awoke the following morning, she woke to a day that was more beautiful than any other day she had ever witnessed. Beauty was everywhere, with the sun shining on the newly bloomed flowers, and the birds chirping as they flitted between the trees and the water fountain.

  She knew in her heart that today would be special. Rising from bed, she knew exactly what she needed to do, although she did not know why. It was as if in a dream she had learned what to do, she made her way as quickly as she could to the foyer where the family tapestries hung telling her family's history. Once amidst their great beauty, she made her way to the old cupboard that now safeguarded the needles and thread that her grandmother and great-grandmother and their mothers before them, had used to create the fine tapestries that told her family's history. Quickly finding what she sought, she placed it within the sleeve of her dress, not really knowing why, but it did bring her comfort to know that it was safely tucked away, knowing that she would have it when she needed it.

Chapter Five

As for the Prince, he saw the castle that same morning well before the villagers saw him, for no longer did the villagers keep a lookout to see what new prince had come to face the three challenges. Over time, everyone had come to realize that no one could pass the Queen's test. Many had tried, but all had failed. Finally, despair ruled, and princes no longer came to their village to seek the hand of the Princess. This Prince, living far from the Princess's village, on the other side of the earth had not heard of the challenge's difficulty, and thinking that all was possible, came with both hope and an open heart.

Reaching the castle gate, the Prince was amazed to find no one there to greet him, not because he was a prince, but because surely many must come to the village to accept the challenge. Stopping at the gate, he waited for someone to approach him, when no one did; he simply walked into the village courtyard. Although weary from his travels, he entered the courtyard standing as tall and honest as a prince should stand. Watching the villagers as they raced about the courtyard, he stood

The Quest

a long time in clothes worn and tattered from the journey, his own thoughts to his own village. Now comforted by the thoughts of home and friends, he set out to explore the village and its people.

Finally, after much walking and watching of the day's activities, he happened upon a young boy jumping in and out of a large puddle. Waiting for the moment he was between jumps, he called out to the boy, "Do you know the way to the Queen's home?"

Somewhere between the leap and the splash, the boy pointed while shouting, "Over there—Sire." After a brief bow, and praise for the boy's jumping and splashing skill, the Prince headed off in the way pointed. Upon reaching the castle, he stopped before the castle's entrance.

No one stopped or greeted him. Standing at the tall broad door of the Queen's palace he paused before reaching for the bell rope. Hesitant at first, he pulled gently expecting to hear the bell's faint chime, but there was no sound and no answer. After waiting a moment more, he pulled harder. Still, the bell was silent and no one came. Unsure whether to enter, he knocked and knocked, which went unanswered. Thinking that something may be wrong or at the least, the bell was broken and his knock went unheard, he found and turned the latch, swung the door open and entered. Gazing throughout the room, which his eyes slowly followed the winding staircase leading up to the foyer's balcony where the vision of the Princess greeted him. His eyes froze and the flowers he held slipped from his hand, and fell to the floor. His lips moved, but no sound came forth.

"Sir, may I be of help, you seem to have caught and

dropped your flowers," came a sweet and friendly voice from the top of the stairs.

Lost in her beauty, he was unable to move until she was close enough to touch. Only then, after kneeling before the Princess did he remember her words about the flowers. Gathering them together, he rose to find the Princess's face mere inches from his own. Bringing the flowers to her hands, he knelt once more and spoke, "Dear Princess, although a prince, I am here as your loyal servant to accept the challenge seeking your hand in marriage. Please bring your servant to your mother, the Queen." Standing once again, and offering yet another bow to the Princess, the Prince's trembling hand reached out to meet the Princess's hand which also trembled at his touch.

Months had passed since the last prince stood before the Queen to hear the first challenge, and she was no more pleased to see this prince than she was the first. *When will they stop coming? No one can complete the challenges I have laid out. When will they stop trying to take my daughter from me? When will they stop bringing danger to her life?* Nevertheless, there he stood, as confident as the first and unprepared for the failure that all the rest had been forced to accept.

Yet, he was unlike all the princes that had come before. He was different. He looked at her daughter the Princess differently, and the Princess looked at him in a way that the Queen had not seen her look at the others. The Princess gazed upon him more kindly than the others, and she had looked kindly on all of them. It was a look that the Queen could not help but notice, and it only made her more concerned and sure that he too must fail the challenge and never return. No one before had made her fear her daughter's safety as much as the young prince who now stood before her.

The Queen spoke. "I have little time today. This must be brief. But first tell me who you are?"

He bowed with his eyes still fixed upon those of the Princess. "Your Majesty, I am a prince who has traveled many weeks to stand before you as your loyal servant, with nothing to offer but the flowers I found growing wild along my travels and have already offered your daughter. Flowers which I first thought beautiful until I saw them near her. I am here to accept the challenges whatever they may be, so that I may prove myself worthy to ask for your daughter's hand in marriage."

"You must be brave indeed to accept a challenge not yet heard. But we have yet to learn if you are also worthy," spoke the Queen. "Here is your first challenge. On the day my daughter was born, what words did my dear dead husband speak to me." Staring dark and deep into the Prince's eyes, she spoke once again, "Return when you know the answer. Take all the time you need, but do not return without the answer. Now go!"

With those final words, the Queen rose from her chair and left without another word, leaving only a brief moment for the Prince and Princess to speak with one another. Gazing into each other's eyes, both knew that they had spent all their young lives waiting for the other, knowing that they loved each other even before they had ever met. Their dreams had come true.

It was only after he bid farewell to the Princess with a bow and left the village, did a heavy gloom settle over him. How could he answer a challenge that asked what was said years ago? He was not there. Who, other than the Queen and King would know? The King was long dead and the Queen was long past telling. His mood darkened, until it became as dark as the lengthening shadows that marked the day's end. Walking back to camp where his friends waited, his sadness was so overwhelming that he took little notice of the tiny holes scattered amidst the soft sand that appeared to be silently following him as he hurried to be with his friends.

Barely able to hold his head high, he entered the camp where his friends waited for him. Upon seeing him, both Brewster and Duncan shouted out a greeting, "When do we meet the Princess?"

Standing quietly off to the side, deep in thought, stood Otis, who had already heard the challenge spoken by the Queen but had not told his brothers. Lost in his own deep thoughts, Otis did not hear the Prince's reply, "I'm afraid, dear friends, you will never get to meet the Princess. But believe me, she is indeed a great beauty, and kind of heart."

Although sad and troubled, over the challenge he believed could never be solved, the Prince told his friends about the day that was quickly ending. First, he told them about the village and the young boy jumping in puddles, even showing them the mud splashes on the cuffs of his pants. He told them about the Princess's great beauty and how the flowers he brought to the Princess had stood taller when she held them, and then he told them the about the first of the three challenges. While telling them about the impossible task, the Prince struggled to hold tight his hope, but holding tight was difficult with hope slipping away.

After listening to all told by the Prince, and saying little, Otis finally spoke. "Although it is not my custom to listen when people talk, and that which I do hear, I make a practice to keep to myself, this is different. The Queen herself has put forth the challenge. Perhaps I can help. Sometimes, but not always, if I listen carefully, I hear the echoes of the ages. Maybe if I listen hard enough, I will hear the echo of what the King spoke that day."

Without saying another word, off he went to the highest hill he could find. Sitting on the hill, his legs crossed and his large hands cupped around his even larger ears, one could see him slowing moving his head from side to side—listening.

Hours passed, the sky grew darker, the world quieter, and still Otis sat motionless on the hill with only his head swaying, stopping only occasionally as if he heard that which he sought to hear. The Prince and his brothers called to him to come and rest, but he would not leave his post. More time passed until his brothers and the Prince could no longer remain awake.

Long into the night, and after the Prince and his brothers were sleeping, Otis could still be found sitting atop the hill with his hands cupped to his ears. When morning broke, the Prince's eyes opened to find the giant standing before him, "I have heard the King's words, and the answer to the challenge." Not waiting to hear more, but trusting his friend, he jumped from his sleep and prepared for his trip back to the castle.

The journey back to the castle passed quickly, for the Prince was far more lighthearted than when he had last left. Yet, as he drew closer and closer to the castle, the Prince could not help but sense that a darkening doom hovered not far from his thoughts. Feeling that brought back the words of the slow-walking man. But, like his dreams, the more he thought of it, the more it seemed to slip away. Thinking as he walked, he walked faster and faster, as if guided by an unseen force drawing him closer and closer to the castle. Lost in thought, the villagers spotted him long before he saw them standing on top of the castle walls.

Although each prince accepting the first challenge had brought hope to the village, this prince created more hope than other princes, for he was the first prince to return a second time. Quickly, the village was abuzz with chatter, and it was not long before all could see the Princess looking from her secret window in her secret room.

"I'm sure that he has found the answer. I just know it."

"No way, no one could ever learn the answer to such a question."

These words were all that could be heard in the village, as the Prince approached from a great

The Quest

distance. As he drew nearer someone said, "He sure looks like he knows." The crowd murmured more and more,

"He knows, he knows," began to ring out among the villagers that lined the castle gate as the Prince drew closer.

This time the Prince had no trouble finding his way to the palace, for the villagers had lined both sides of a path straight to the Queen's door. The Prince found the Queen standing in the foyer of the castle with the Guard Captain, but the Queen was not whom the Prince hoped to see. He tried to listen to the Queen, while also seeking to catch a glimpse of the Princess. He was not doing very well at either task. Finally, he spotted her, close to where he had seen her for the very first time. There she was, standing on the stairs, clutching the flowers, which he had brought her.

Hearing his name in a voice that sounded as if he was being scolded, he turned back to face the Queen. "Prince, you must either be indeed worthy if you have answered the challenge or foolish to return without an answer, and I think you more foolish than worthy."

"Dear Queen, do you wish me to speak here among your villagers?"

"Speak now, Prince. There are no finer villagers anywhere. Answer me here among the people who love the Princess most. What did my husband say to me the day our daughter was born?"

"Your husband spoke many words that day, words that a loving husband would speak to his wife the day she gave birth to a beautiful daughter, and those words will remain between the two of you—always. However, the words that I believe you wish to hear are, 'Look wife, look at the lovely pearl necklace I have had crafted for our infant daughter. Years from now I will place them around her neck the day she is married.'"

The people gathered in the courtyard froze and a hush fell among the room. They all held their breath waiting for the Queen to speak. No one could be sure whether these were the correct words. Were these the words that the Queen did not wish to hear from any prince?

The Queen brought her hand to her mouth, as if to stop the tiny gasp, which she could not stop from escaping her lips. Finally, turning to her right, she called her daughter to come and join her. As the Prince watched the Princess glide down the stairs, everyone else's eyes fixed on the Queen.

When the Princess was close enough to take her mother's hand, the Queen spoke, "You have indeed proven yourself worthy for no other prince has ever returned with the correct answer. Now we must see if you are worthy still. For your second challenge, you must answer the following. Upon my husband's death, I took and hid the necklace. Where is it hidden?" As the words left her mouth, she quickly turned and walked off with the Princess in tow. Although the Queen walked out of the room without speaking another word, both the young Princess and the Queen paused long enough to briefly catch the Prince's eyes before the palace door slammed shut.

Chapter Six

While more confident than his first trip back from the castle to where he and his friends had camped, the Prince knew that this challenge was more difficult than the first. Words may echo through the ages, but something hidden must first be found and that was beyond even what he believed his new friends could accomplish, for no one could see through the walls that might safeguard the hidden necklace he sought from view.

Lost in thought, he almost failed to notice the small holes that once again appeared before him. Seeing them once more, and feeling the chill they brought to his body, he wondered why he had not mentioned them to his friends. Then redoubling his steps, he made haste to reach his friends before the sun dimmed from orange to red. As fast as he walked, he still could not help but think that his hopes were dimming faster than the sun's light.

Returning to camp with thoughts of the impossible challenge before him—he entered with a sadness far removed from the day's earlier happiness. Although worried about the difficulty of the second challenge, he entered camp smiling and waving; not wanting to appear ungrateful for all the help the giants had already given him. He found his friends hovering over a large simmering kettle that had filled the air with a wonderful aroma long before he had seen it. Jumping up upon seeing him and nearly knocking the kettle over, they paid it no mind for they were eager to learn of the Prince's meeting with the Queen.

The Prince told the three of the second challenge, and as he talked of this new and difficult test, the more his mood darkened over the difficulty of this second challenge.

Sensing his deepening gloom, Duncan his large eyes twinkling in the setting sunlight softly spoke, "Friend, are you losing hope yet again? Do not despair. My brothers and I began this quest at your side, and we will not leave your side until it is done. Find the necklace we must, find it we will. Now it is my turn to help in the search."

With his words still ringing among the mountains that surrounded their camp, Duncan walked off to the same hill that Otis had spent the evening before. However, this time he did it by day and not night, for whereas the quiet of the night is best for listening, the bright light of day is best for seeing.

There he sat, his eyes slowly turning in all directions, as if his eyes were a lighthouse casting a long light upon that which could not be seen before. Never a word escaped his lips, not a shout of joy nor a gasp of disappointment. Rather, he attended to his task, confident that with time he would find the necklace, no matter how long he had to search.

When the others asked him to join them for supper, all he did was shake his head back and forth, continuing the search even with his silent answer. Only after the sun had set and all was dark, did Duncan join his brothers and the Prince. Even then, it was only for a quick bite, and off he went to sleep so that his eyes would be well rested to begin his search with the first light of day.

Long after daybreak had come that morning, the Prince, Brewster, and Otis, awoke to find Duncan sitting with his elbows on his knees, with both a quiet smile and a look of concern showing on his face, as he waited my for them to rustle from their sleep. At first, Duncan said nothing, but all knew that he was waiting for his companions to ask if he had found success, which none did.

"I guess it's time to make breakfast," said the Prince, while Brewster stretched and toyed with his beard, and Otis yawned tugging at his ear.

"Do you not have something to ask of me," Duncan excitedly asked.

"No, No, No." came three quick answers.

"Are you not interested to hear where it is hidden?"

"No, not really, maybe later" was heard three times—one after another after another.

Finally, the Prince too excited to continue with the teasing, asked, "Yes, tell us what you have found—have you truly found where the necklace is hidden?"

"Yes, yes indeed, I have found the necklace, but first we must talk."

Once Duncan had spoken about the need to

talk, Otis found himself also saying, "Yes, we must talk." Once Otis had announced the need to talk, Brewster and the Prince knew that there must be much to discuss, since both knew that Otis was far more comfortable listening than talking, and if Otis meant to talk, it must be important. So, they gathered around the morning fire, quietly thinking and eating, but doing more thinking than eating.

When the time was ready to talk, Duncan spoke first. He told of finding the necklace, hidden deep beneath a great sea. He also told about what else lied near the undisturbed necklace, which told that many men had tried to recover it from the deep sea and failed. When it was Otis's turn to speak, he began by telling all he had heard when he had listened for the King's words and had kept secret until now. Once the four friends had heard all of what had been said long ago by Otis, and all that had been seen beneath the sea by Duncan, the evil now known, became darker and darker.

Once Otis and Duncan had spoken, all began to speak to what it might mean, what needed to be done, and how they would overcome the evil, which they had found along with the necklace. But, as much as their knowledge brought them success, all felt a deep sorrow for the Queen for she had carried the heaviest burden, one more difficult than even the three challenges. They could not help but be moved by the sorrow the Queen had been forced to carry deep within her spirit.

While listening to all that was being said, the Prince found his thoughts drifting away, thinking that he had part of the story that was now understanding

The Quest

being told. But, as hard as he tried to remember, his memory was always just out of reach. Could his forgotten thoughts and the story now being told be connected? Was it part of the challenge, was it a different challenge, or, were they different parts of the same challenge? It was a most unsettling feeling and as much as he wanted to share his feelings with his friends. he could not find the words to describe them. Yet, he knew this evil; their paths had crossed before—once recently, and once long ago.

All that day was spent talking, trying to understand how difficult it must be for the Princess and the Queen, and how the Queen suffered her pain alone as she fearfully waited for danger to raise its terrible hand yet again. It was now clear that over the years, everyone had buried their fear and pain, even the Guard Captain kept his thoughts hidden and his lips sealed. Fear had locked the secret tight, in the hope that by hiding their fear and never speaking of it, the Princess might be safe. A fear so frightening and hidden so deeply that now it had been forgotten, by all but the Queen and the Guard Captain.

After much talking, but still uncertain of all they had learned, they retired for the evening. The long night dragged on slowly, each knowing that the others were not sleeping, but no words more could be spoken. Yet, the fear of what was to come, spoke often to the Prince in his dreams. Arising the next morning, even less was said over breakfast than dinner. Slowly, the Prince prepared for his journey back to the castle, once again thinking there was something he meant to tell his friends. But the more he thought of it, the more it slipped away.

Bidding his friends farewell once again, the Prince found himself retracing his steps as he walked towards the castle, a path well worn by his own footsteps. But there was something more, something close to his own footsteps, which he could not understand—the tiny holes which lied scattered among the soft sand. Even with the knowledge that the slow-walking man had shared with him, he could still not understand their meaning. Seeing them again, he remembered that he had forgotten to mention them to his friends. Remembering to remember to tell his friends, he continued his journey back to the Castle.

While each trip found him more confident having now answered two challenges, each time also found him more wary of what new challenge will have to be answered. Yet, that was a feeling he understood, it was the haunting feeling that hovered over him, especially now that the reason for the challenges was clearer to him. That troubled him the most. A mystery that the Prince could only feel, but not yet understand, one that seemed to linger just outside of sight. Most troubling was that he was sure that if he turned his head quick enough, he would find evil lingering nearby. It was never quite there when he turned his head.

Unafraid of what was to come, his journey back was marked with joy and anticipation as well as apprehension—joy and anticipation to see the Princess and apprehension that the Queen would ask the impossible. Joy and apprehension were feelings he could understand, what he could not understand, was when his thoughts would turn to the tiny holes that dotted his path and could never remember to mention to his friends. Drawing nearer to the castle, he scanned the windows and the castle walkways that surrounded the village for a glimpse of the Princess.

He was not to be disappointed. It was easy to find the Princess standing in the window high above the village, for no window beckoned more to his heart. Walking quickly, closer and closer he neared the castle, never once taking his eyes off those of the Princess, until he saw her drop a note, which tumbled and turned its way to his waiting hands. Opening the letter, it did not take him long to read. Then, carefully folding the letter, he slipped it inside the secret pocket, nearest his heart, which the tailor had stitched into his shirt. Looking up once again, the Princess had vanished from the window, but now he noticed that the entire village lined the walkways and filled every window of the village.

Little was said among the villagers once the Prince had been spied returning, most did not know what to say or even what to think. No one could believe that the Prince had returned with the first challenge answered, to see him return a second time was too much for anyone to accept. The village stood still as if time had stopped. Everyone was frozen in place as the Prince walked among them, only stepping aside to let him pass.

The first person that the Prince recognized was the young boy he met on his first visit jumping in and out of puddles. Now, here he was hurrying to bring him a ladle of water to quench his thirst.

Looking over the head of the approaching boy, his eyes fell upon the castle door, to see the person he longed most to see—the Princess. As the Princess approached, his hand moved to his shirt where her note laid close to his heart.

Before the Prince even had time to bow, the Princess took the ladle filled with water from the young boy, touched his head, and while handing the ladle to the Prince, announced in a voice loud enough for all to hear, "We are indeed fortunate to have you grace us with you presence once again. Come, follow me, we shall see my mother the Queen together." Taking his hand, she turned and guided him through the maze of people gathered to await his answer.

The walk back to the castle was cut short, when the crowd opened and the Prince and Princess found themselves standing before the Queen. Letting go the Princess's hand, the Prince bowed before the Queen and spoke. "Your Majesty, I have returned to answer the second of your three challenges. Shall I speak here and now?"

Standing among her people, the Queen was no less astonished than they were as she looked upon the Prince standing before her. No mighty warrior wearing armor and battle tested weapons, he was a simple man, yet still a prince. Although not yet willing to admit that she was beginning to like this young man, she did speak to him far less harshly than she had the first and second time he stood before her. This time, she spoke in an almost kind voice, "Seeker of my daughter's hand, tell me, have you learned where I hid the necklace."

"Yes, yes I have learned where it lays hidden. But, before I speak, I must be truthful, I was only able to learn the answer to your challenge through the kindness and help of others, whom, without their help I would not have been able to answer these two challenges."

Looking at the Prince as if to peer into his heart, the Queen replied, "Such help would only be given to someone worthy of their help. Those offering help know you best, should they wish to help bring happiness to you and the Princess, they do so out of affection for you. It matters not that you receive help, but remember, there remains yet another challenge. Now, before you hear the third challenge, answer me what I asked."

Taking back the Princess's hand in his own, he spoke only part of the answer that Duncan had given him and he had carried to the Queen. "In anguish and sadness over the death of your husband the King and fear for your daughter's safety, you dropped the necklace into the deepest part of the sea between the two towering mountains which separate the sea never crossed, where it still lies today."

Emotion did not escape the Queen, as she looked at first the Prince and then the Princess. The Prince watched the Princess, while the Princess searched her mother's face to learn if this Prince had truly answered the challenge. Beyond this circle stood the villagers, each one sure at first he was wrong, then equally sure that he was right, and then back again wrong, then right, then wrong, until none knew what to think. All they could do was search the Queen's face for a clue.

Time ticked on, and only the ticking of the castle clock broke the silence that had fallen upon the town square. Tick-tock, tick, tock, they waited, all straining to see whatever they could see and hear whatever they could hear. Finally, the silence was broken by the young boy known for his jumping in and out of puddles. Hollering from the castle walk high above the town square he asked, "Well, is he right or wrong? When are you going to tell us?"

Knowing from whom and where the voice came from, the Queen could not help but smile, and with that smile, people began to notice a change. What they saw was their Queen looking first at the Prince, then her daughter, then the villagers, and back to the Prince. What they did not know is what the Queen was thinking. If they had, they would have known that their Queen, for the first time ever, was unsure what to do next.

She knew that the last of the three tasks would bring danger to the Prince and now becoming quite fond of him, she feared for his safety, but she had to be sure. She had to be convinced that her daughter would be safe now and in the future; she had to know if danger still lurked for her daughter. Only the successful completion of the third and final challenge would bring peace to her heart. Yet, in her mind, the Queen now feared that finding the necklace would not only put the Prince in peril, but also her daughter, whom she had sought to protect.

However, as much as she wished to keep her daughter safe, she could not help but worry about the Prince's safety. She knew that evil does not simply vanish.

The Quest

When it was that the silence could not last a second longer, the Queen finally spoke, "Prince, each time we meet, I become more at ease with your simple manner. Never boastful, never too proud to look lovingly at my daughter, even now after you have correctly answered the second challenge, your only concern is hearing of the final challenge."

If the town square had been quiet moments before, now even the clock had stopped ticking. No sound was heard as the Queen's words settled in among the villagers. Each villager searched the eyes of the person standing closest to make sure that what they had heard was really true. No one moved, everyone in the village held their breath waiting for the Queen to speak again, the only movement was the Princess squeezing tight the Prince's hand as her heart raced with joy.

As quickly as quiet had descended upon the town moments earlier, now that the villagers were sure that the Prince spoke the truth, the town burst into dancing and cheering just as quickly. The only ones not moving were the Princess, and Queen, the ever-loyal Captain of the Guard, and the Prince quietly awaiting word of the third challenge while the Princess held tight his hand. Standing opposite them was the Queen, trying to balance her heavy heart, knowing that only by placing the young Prince in peril could she free her daughter from the danger, which always lurked nearby, just out of sight.

Raising her hand, the Queen called for silence so she could speak with the Prince. No second request was necessary for the entire village wanted to hear of the third task.

Quiet once again settled over the village square until the silence was broken by the Prince, "Your Majesty, please place the third challenge before me."

Looking more kindly than anyone could remember, the Queen walked to where the Prince stood and taking his hand spoke, "Son, it is with a heavy heart that I tell you the third challenge. Never thinking that any man could complete the first two, I never gave thought to the danger it presented. Should you decide to accept this challenge, my thoughts go with you. Should you decide not to accept, my thoughts also go with you. Think hard before you accept, and know that whatever you decide you will always be remembered."

"Your concern for my safety brings joy to my heart, your thoughts strength; now tell me, what is the third and final challenge?"

The Queen squeezing his hand even tighter for a long time, finally spoke, "You are to bring the necklace to me, so that my daughter can wear it on her wedding day."

Returning the Queen's affectionate squeeze, he then let go her hand, and removed his father's ring from his finger, the most cherished of all his belongings. Turning to the Princess, he then placed the ring in her hand, and whispering so that she alone might hear what he said, "Keep this safe till I return, lest I lose it retrieving your necklace."

Taking the ring from his hand, her hand lingered a moment longer as she replaced the ring

The Quest

with the tiny satchel that she had taken from the tapestry room and kept tucked within her sleeve for just this moment. Then standing on her toes, she leaned forwarded and whispered into his ear, so that only he could hear, "And I have something for you. Please take this, ask me not why I give it to you, I myself do not know why—I just know that I must give it to you, and you must take it. It is what ties our future to the past. Guard it safely for me. Use it as you will, for you are the one who is meant to have it." Then, in a quieter voice, she spoke once again, for no one else to hear.

Once the ring was safely in the Princess's hand, and the satchel the Princess have given him was lying along side her note, in the secret pocket, he turned back to the Queen and spoke, "When I return, your fears will be washed away, your heart lighter, and your daughter safe." Then, bowing first to the Princess, and then the Queen, and even to the villagers, he wrapped his cape around himself and checking to find the Princess's letter and satchel still near his heart, turned to begin his quest for the third and final challenge, leaving everyone to ponder the meaning of his words.

Chapter Seven

After walking till he could no longer see the castle, he stopped and sat for a long while. Running through his mind, over and over, were the words that Duncan had told him about where the necklace lay hidden, "Buried deep beneath the cold dead sea, surrounded by death, and twice as deep as my tallest brother." Putting aside his own feelings of love for the Princess and desire to free the Queen from her burden, he could not allow his friends to risk their life for him.

Lost in thought, the Prince almost failed to notice the tiny holes that once again followed him in the dimming light. Seeing the darkening sky fall upon the land, he resumed walking so that he would arrive before nightfall. One foot after another, after another, one step after another, trying to concentrate on his walking, still he was unable to shake fear from his mind. A fear that had no name, one that he could not even explain to his friends. There was another fear, however, one that he could understand. This was a fear for his friend's safety, for he knew that his friends would stay by his side until the challenges were completed—their word once given—they would never walk away now. He must find a way to spare his friends, especially Brewster, who ever since the first challenge was known, had said that the final challenge was his to help.

The Prince knew that no amount of thanks would convince Brewster that without him, he would not have reached the castle, or met his brothers, or had the courage to carry on the quest. But, he also knew and feared that nothing he could say would stop him from trying to reach the necklace, risking his own life. No matter how much he tried to forget what Duncan had told him laid near the necklace, the image brought fear for his friend's safety, a fear which ran deeper than even the great depth where the necklace had been hidden. Over and over, a single question consumed his thoughts. *Would it not be better to miss out on the greatest love in all the world and and not risk his friend's life? Or could he take a chance that might bring a premature end to it? But, if I and my friends do nothing, how else could we help the Princess?* His thoughts ran in circles, *what happiness could come from such a love if it was at the expense of his dear friend?* But how else could he help the Princess?

More and more, his thoughts turned from a Princess bride to how he could keep his friends safe while also freeing the Princess and the Queen from fear and danger. Never before had he been faced with such a decision. A decision that a king would find difficult, to say nothing of a prince, and yet, he kept asking himself, "Don't all men and woman face and conquer challenges never believed imaginable?"

His thoughts kept going back to his parents. How he wished they were there to help him. He also wondered if the Princess was spinning and twisting his father's ring, as he would often do, when faced with a difficult choice, or when he missed his parents. On he walked, troubled, tired, and weary, but as the miles disappeared, so did his doubt. No Prince can risk the life of another for his own happiness. Princes served their people and they put their life at risk before they would ask others to do the same. That is what his father the King had always told him. If someone must retrieve the necklace, it would be him. He did not know how, and he knew he would need help, but he would not risk the safety of his loyal friends. Comfortable with his decision, his step became lighter and it was not too long before he was home among his friends. And yet the tiny holes that once again shadowed his steps, brought a swelling fear upon him.

Seeing him approach from a distance, his friends rose to greet him, greatly interested in what he had to say, since completing the final challenge was now as important to them as it was to the Prince. "What is the next challenge?" came their collective shout—making it difficult to hear a single voice amidst the chorus.

Seeing their excitement, and sensing their willingness to help, he now realized that refusing their help was more complicated than he had thought on his walk home. The Prince now realized that helping others is what made his friends the happiest—fighting dragons, answering challenges, doing what no one else could do is what fulfilled them. Thinking back to when their journey together had begun, he realized how their moods had changed. They talked more, laughed more, they were more light-hearted, and shared more of their lives with each step.

Now, it was the Prince who rose last each morning, only to find fire and breakfast already prepared and three giants ready to face the new day. Finally, after noticing that all three of his friends had been staring at him eagerly waiting to hear what he had to say, the Prince could only utter, "I must think, friends, I must think." What he did not say aloud, and what even Otis could not hear, continued to ring within his head, "Do I have the right to risk their safety, even if they are willing to risk their lives?"

***

Watching from a distance, the three brothers had never heard or seen him look so distressed. Knowing that the Prince must be hungry from his long walk, even if he did not know it, they brought him food and drink they had prepared while he was gone. After a quiet dinner, with not much spoken other than, "pass this, or pass that," the Prince walked off to the same high hill where Duncan and Otis had found their answers, where, he thought, he might be able to find his answers. Sitting alone on the hill, he would often look to see his friends talking, and know that he could never ask one, or any of them, to risk danger for his sake.

As dusk slowly turned to night, Brewster

and Duncan began to look more and more closely at Otis. It was easy to see that Otis knew what was troubling the Prince, for he had been the quietest of the three throughout the long afternoon. Finally, his patience exhausted, Brewster announced, "I'm getting to the bottom of this. Duncan, you and I are the only two who still don't know, and we must know if we are to help." Calling to the Prince, "Prince, come down from the hill and sit with us—speak to us as friends. We stand together, all of us. Now come here, and tell us of the challenge and why you are so troubled. We will help; no challenge is stronger than the four of us. Now trust us with your troubles."

Although a Prince, it was hard to refuse the request of a giant, especially when he has two brothers that are also giants. Heartened by their constant friendship and concern, and hearing Brewster's confidence that together they could conquer all, the Prince began to think that maybe together they could find a way. Huddled together around what remained of the evening fire, it looked much like any other night they had spent together. Yet, all knew that tonight was different, and morning would be different still.

After looking at the stars, all hoping that an answer might fall from the sky, Brewster, after coughing once or twice, finally spoke. "What is it of this third challenge that troubles you so, friend?"

"Yes, what is it?" echoed Duncan.

Only Otis did not speak, and Brewster found himself turning to his brother Otis and saying, "And, yes, Brother Otis, Duncan and I already know that you know what was said, so what say you?"

Knowing the third challenge already, Otis could only turn to the Prince and say, "Friend, why are you so troubled, are we not here to help you?"

As they stared waiting for his response, the Prince began to tell them of the day that had just passed. He spoke of the Princess's beauty and how pleased she was to be given his father's ring for safekeeping, and the gift she had given to him. He spoke of the Queen's kind words, and how he longed to free her from worry. When he knew that Brewster and Duncan could wait no longer, he told them that returning the necklace to its true owner, the Princess, was the third challenge. He waited for them to say something, knowing that they shared his concern over the difficulty of the task. Thinking that he would have to wait longer, he was surprised to hear the brothers in perfect unity say, "We start in the morning."

"Wait!" said the Prince. "It has not been decided." Taking a moment before speaking, since he did not want to offend, he went on, "I cannot ask one, or any of my friends to risk their lives for me. If someone is to go down to the depths of the ocean, it will be me. It is my challenge. It is true that without your help, I never would have reached the third challenge, but now that I have, the final challenge is mine. The risk is also mine. It is mine alone. I will not pass this risk to you, I will not allow you to risk harm to yourselves. Now—now it is decided."

The Prince's three friends looked at one

another and then looked at him, and then Brewster spoke. "Dear friend, we will not be risking our lives for someone who would not do the same for one of us. Is that not true? When we were lost, lost because we believed no one needed our help, your quest gave our lives meaning. Why would we not be willing to risk our lives for someone who has returned meaning to our lives? Even if it is as dangerous as you say, and it may not be as dangerous for a giant such as me, only I can decide what risk I will take for a friend. Are not friends willing to risk all that they possess, their lives included, to help a friend, a loved one, a child, or for even a stranger in need of help? It is not only princes that possess a noble heart. We, all three of us, may be giants, but our hearts are like the one that beats in you. Let us help. You have helped us, you have taught us and we have learned that helping others is what makes us giants. Our fathers knew that all too well, but they did not change in a changing world. They thought that they could help only by slaying dragons, and once the last dragon was gone, there was little they could do from that day onward. With your help, we have learned that generosity is not measured by the size of the help, but the size of one's heart."

After a long silence, with only the crackling fire making a sound, Brewster, in a more light-hearted tone, spoke once more, "We wish to do this for you, and the Princess we have yet to meet. We do have one request. Never in all our travels have we met anyone who carries our name. When the day comes that you and the Princess have children, if the Princess agrees, you have our permission to name your children after us—starting with me first." If it were not for the smile that Brewster's last words brought to everyone's lips, not much would have been said for a long, long, time. His words may have been simple, but one could not find disagreement with a single word. So, there they sat, without a word being spoken, each thinking of the journey that had bonded their friendship, each knowing that no better friends could be found anywhere at anytime.

Finally, unable to wait any longer, Brewster stood and in a sure voice spoke, "Good, it is decided, we will go down to sea at the first light of day, and I, with my long arms and legs will search until I find the necklace. We need sleep now, for tomorrow will be the most difficult of our days together." Looking at Brewster, all that the Prince, Otis, and Duncan could do was to nod a silent yes.

Having settled in for the long evening, lying between two trees, safe from Duncan's tossing and turning, the Prince could not help but believe that someone was watching over him, since no one man could have such good friends. Yet, as he moved closer and closer to success, he sometimes thought it was not only good that was watching over him. There was always something more, along with the good, an unwavering sense that evil was also accompanying him on his journey.

His mind racing, sleep did not come easy for the Prince. Lying beneath the stars, listening to the fire crackle as it slowly burnt itself out, he could not help but wonder, why had he even with his friend's help, been able to find the Princess and complete the challenges. All he could think was that his success had more to do with the help of his villagers, a slow-walking man, and three giants than it had to do with him. While the Prince knew many of the people whom he had to thank, what the Prince did not know was that a young Princess, long before he had met her, half-a-world away at the moment he began his journey, caught a falling star and made a wish. Struggling to keep hope alive in his heart, and the wish that by the end of their journey together, all would be safe, he finally drifted off to sleep.

It was still dark when Duncan shook the Prince from his sleep, "Wake, for there is enough light to begin our journey. Let us begin now, and we will have breakfast when the sun rises." Lacing his once-new shoes, he noticed that they were now as scuffed and worn as the shoes that the slow-walking man had worn the day he arrived at his village. Once they were laced, he reached for a nearby branch, which had escaped the evening's fire, to pull himself up. As he did so, while still looking at his shoes, he noticed something that he had seen before in the soft sand.

But before he could give it any thought, Brewster announced, "No time for walking, today you ride." With that, Brewster reached down, and hastily grabbing him by the collar, picked him up and placed him on his shoulder. Now, looking at his brothers over his shoulder where the Prince sat, Brewster spoke in a strong, clear voice, "The journey will be long. If we hurry, we can reach the great sea by sundown and search the following morning. Are we agreed?"

"Yes," was all the Prince answered, knowing that Brewster would have it no other way, but it did little to ease the ache that his heart felt over risking his friend's safety. But there was something more, as if he had missed something important, something that was right there, but that he couldn't see.

Chapter Eight

The trip was easier than all had thought, for although it was a great distance to the sea, the path had been made easy by the smooth sand that was left behind as the sea grew smaller and the world larger. When they had arrived, the sun was still shining, but the Prince insisted that they wait for morning, when they would be better rested. Although the Prince saw danger when he looked out upon the great sea for the first time, it still held great beauty. Sitting beside the great sea, the two soaring mountains stood exactly as Duncan had described, and it was not difficult to imagine that they were standing guard to protect the necklace.

Hearing his name called, he turned to find Brewster joining him as he, too, sat upon the cool sand. Together they sat, without saying a word, scanning the horizon and watching the waves lap gently upon the shore. Deep in thought, it was difficult for the Prince to imagine that such a beautiful sea with its gentle swaying and cool breeze would soon bring great peril to his friend.

Sensing the Prince's concern, Brewster spoke, "Friend, I will be fine and I will emerge safely from the sea holding the Princess's necklace. Nothing will stop me from returning safely."

Although Brewster's words echoed for a long time in the air, ebbing softer and softer into the dark night, the Prince did not say a word. Turning to the young prince, Brewster noticed the Prince's long hair now fell upon his face. Brewster did not have to look too closely before he knew that the Prince's hair masked the tears that spilled from his eyes. Always the friend, Brewster moved closer to the Prince, his eyes gazing upon the same sea that lay beyond the Prince's tear-clouded eyes.

Finally, after countless waves had caressed the shore beyond where they sat, Brewster placed his massive arm behind his small friend's back. "Friend, you sit here in sorrow thinking of what your quest might take from your friends, and yet you don't think of all you have given to me and my brothers. If you did, you would know that you have given far more than your task can ever take." Not understanding, the Prince turned to his friend, but said nothing. Yet, it was clear to both of them that the Prince did not understand his friend's meaning.

There they sat, watching the sun slip between the two towering mountains until it dipped beneath the sea. As the sky darkened, and the moon rose, Brewster began speaking yet again. "Look, look up at the stars. Do you see the two falcons resting on a tree branch. Do you see the larger one passing its talon brimming with food to the smaller one?" Although the Prince peered into the night sky, he did not see what his friend spoke of seeing. Finally, turning to his friend with a look of having disappointed someone dear to him, he admitted he could not see the two falcons or even the tree branch upon which they sat.

Returning his friend's disappointed look with one of fondness, Brewster spoke. "Friend, do not despair. You may not see it now, but someday you will."

"How can that be?" replied the Prince. "If I do not see it today, how can I see it tomorrow, or the day after? Tell me again, which stars make up the twin falcons. Point them out to me. Show them to me again."

Smiling, Brewster spoke, "Better yet, give me that stick, I will make points in the sand for each star, but you will still not see the falcons."

"How can that be, if you see them, then they are there for all to see."

"No friend, while they may be there for me, they are not yet there for you."

Feeling more confused than he had ever felt before, the Prince turned to his friend and said, "Brewster, you speak in riddles. How can it be there for you, and not for me? Do we not look at the same stars?"

"Yes, yes we do, but it is our hearts, our thoughts, and our experiences that are different. I look at you, and I see your gifts, gifts that you yourself do not see within yourself. These are the strengths that I know you possess, and I am sure that they will emerge when they are called upon. That is your inner strength. That is why you look upon the morning challenge with fear for me, your friend. I look upon the challenge as helping you, helping me and helping my brothers. You fail to see the gifts you possess. Do you not know that you have brought my brothers and me together? Do you not realize that after tomorrow you will bring love and happiness to a Princess and freedom from fear for the Queen? Sometimes we see, but we don't understand. Sometimes, because we do not understand the past, we do not see what lies before our very eyes."

Once more, the Prince looked closely at Brewster, his face questioning all that had been said. "Fear not, my friend, you will understand soon enough. Now, put aside your worry, for it is time we sleep."

***

The Prince was not the only one worried, for as he and his friends were about to seek sleep, there were others just rising from their beds having slept little. Both the Queen and the Princess had spent the evening trying to sleep, only to rise often from their beds to gaze upon a darkened sky in hope of seeing some sign that the Prince was safe. Each trip to the window, however, brought little solace, and each returned to bed without finding the answer, more worried than before they had sought him through the window. Even that slumber, which did sneak into the Princess and Queen's sleepless night, was driven away and shattered by their frightful dreams.

Each night was the same for the Queen and Princess since the Prince's last visit and his hoped for return, and each night, as the Princess and Queen retired to their rooms, standing between the two doors stood the Guard Captain. Never knowing the comfort of his own bed, the Guard Captain stood faithful watch. It was not fear of strangers that he could see which made him stand watch, but his love for the two people he knew went without sleep, and a sense that evil now lingered closer than ever. He stood, never tiring, thinking only of his promised duty to his King, and more importantly, his friend.

***

While he stood guard for his long dead friend, two friends, also dear to one another sat quietly upon a distant beach. Finding sleep difficult, they gave up trying and sat without speaking on the shore of the sea, which would challenge them the following morning. After the moon had dropped from the sky, and the night became even darker, Brewster turned to his friend, and spoke, "I will come back. I've got to make sure that you name your first son Brewster."

Leaning over, the Prince, standing as tall as he could, reached and yanked at one of his whiskers, only to make Brewster howl with laughter, which soon spread to Duncan and Otis, and it was not long before all four were howling with delight, their laughter providing needed relief from the peril they would soon face. While Brewster was the one retrieving the necklace, all knew, especially Brewster, that they all went with him into the deep, dark depths of the sea. Comforted by their laughter, they retired to their makeshift beds among the tall trees, hoping that this time they might find solace in their dreams.

The following morning, all woke to a sky filled more with clouds than sun, which brought concern to the Prince, but not to Brewster, or at least he was able to hide his fear for his friend's sake. Speaking more loudly than usual, as if to convince himself, Brewster declared, "Good, the clouds will hide the sun's long shadows under the sea, which will make finding the necklace easy."

No one believed him, but all agreed hoping it would help ease their concern. Lighting the morning fire, all decided that it must be as big as possible, so that it might serve as a beacon should Brewster lose his way deep beneath the sea, or at least they hoped it would help. Final preparations were made and all that was left to do for Brewster was to remove all that was buried deep within his pockets.

Otis, the youngest of all the brothers, could not hide his concern for Brewster's safety and kept saying after taking each object Brewster withdrew from his pocket. "You'll need this upon your return," or "Mustn't lose this, what will you do without it when you get back." Everyone agreed that Brewster would need this or that upon his return, but it did little to hide their fear for Brewster's safety.

When nothing was left to remove from his pockets, Brewster began taking deep breaths and letting the air out slowly. Once, long ago, he had watched a man do it before diving in and remaining under water only to emerge with what looked like many of the shells that lined the water's edge—and then pry them open to remove a small pretty white stone that was hidden within the shell.

Over and over, he did this until he was ready to enter the water. Turning to his brothers and the Prince, he only asked, "Have something to drink and warm to eat when I return. I will be hungry."

Before Brewster could take one more step, the Prince called, "Wait," and then turning to Otis, "Quickly, pick me up so I can speak with Brewster."

Lifted by Otis to where the Prince could look directly at Brewster, he began to speak. "Friend, one final time, you need not do this, there must be another way. Please, do not do this, I fear for your safety. Have you forgotten what Duncan said lies alongside the necklace? I cannot allow this."

"Prince, it has already been decided, and I will return to see you name your child after me. A promise is a promise." With those final words, Brewster turned and began walking into the water. First, his ankles were covered, then his knees were lost to the water, higher and higher, the water rose covering more and more of him. When only his neck and head were still to be seen, he called out, "Not bad, not bad at all." After several more deep breaths, he plunged straight down into the sea, and it was not long before the ripples vanished and the sea was as calm as it was before he entered.

Chapter Nine

Onshore, they waited, each holding their breath, waiting for Brewster to rise from the sea. Brewster's brothers and the Prince remained silent, each counting the moments, all hoping to see a sign that Brewster was safe. Just when they thought that no more time could pass, the water began churning and heaving as if a great storm brewed below the sea. Waves began crashing at their feet; it was hard for them not to think that their hopes were also crashing. Watching the sea churning and rolling, they did what they could do to help. Moving into the cresting waves, they called out "Brewster, Brewster, where are you?"

The waves became higher, the sound of the crashing waves louder, and the sky began to darken. Fighting against fear, and struggling against the waves that pounded their bodies, they fought their way into the sea. Engulfed within the battering waves, Duncan and Otis strode into the sea—where even their powerful legs were pushed back. The Prince labored to stay along side his friends, Otis and Duncan. Pounded by the sea, their clothes had become tattered, their eyes clouded, and their limbs weakened, but still they moved forward. Swamped by the sea, nearly beaten, and near exhaustion, they continued together—when, together, they noticed a change. The waters were becoming calmer, now the sea was only swirling in a single spot.

The sea was no longer angry. The waters were calming, but where was Brewster? They waited, and then rising from the sea, first fingers, then a wrist, an arm, an elbow—Brewster was safe. More and more became visible, until Brewster stood before them, wet, yet safe. There he stood, still with his arm held high over his head, when they saw it. Sparkling white, his hand held the Princess's necklace, once lost and now found; together they had completed the final task.

But the Prince knew, deep in his very being, that danger had not truly passed, although he did not know why or how he knew. There would be another challenge, one that his friends could not be of help, and one not of the Queen's doing. There was to be another struggle, one between good and evil. Yet, this was one day that fear would not win, together, they had done what no one thought possible. Today was a day to celebrate. Tomorrow, and what laid ahead could wait the evening.

In all the excitement, no one remembered that Brewster requested food upon his return, so Duncan and Otis set upon the task, while all warmed themselves by the roaring fire. Although all tried to busy themselves with one task or another, they found it difficult not to look at the necklace. Beautiful, and crafted with the love of a father for his daughter, all that ran through their minds was—how could it have caused so much pain and sorrow?

The Quest

How did it become the center of the three challenges? Finally, it was agreed, it was not the necklace that caused pain; it was the evil of a single man. Evil had not won, at least not today. Now, the necklace could return to what it had always been, a wedding gift from a father to a loved daughter, nothing could erase that ever again.

Sitting around the fire, it was not long before all were dry, well fed and joyful over what they had achieved. Still, words did not come easy. No one needed to say it, but all knew that with the completion of the final challenge their quest together was over. Silently they sat, each knowing in their hearts that the Prince was to face a new struggle. What no one knew, what no one could be sure of, was where and when.

Finally, Duncan spoke, "In the morning, dear friend, we will walk with you towards the castle as far as camp, and then, my brothers and I will say our goodbye, and you will walk the rest of the way to the castle."

"No, you must return with me to the castle, you and your brothers began this quest at my side, you will be there when it is ended. You must come and meet the Princess. She must meet my three dear friends; friends who have helped me win her hand." Although the Prince truly wanted them to join him, he sensed that this was the way that it must come to pass. There was to be another challenge, one that he must face—alone.

Otis, realizing that Duncan had not the heart to refuse a request, answered—"No, tomorrow will be your day, you must go alone. When you enter the village, all eyes must be upon you. All must know you are the one who has won the Princess's hand and freed her mother from any more sleepless nights. You are the Prince that the village has long waited. You must go alone."

Before the Prince could reply, it was Brewster's turn to talk, "We must be off, not because we do not wish to stand beside you, rather, we must begin our own quest. You have planted the seeds of our new life; we must learn new ways to help. That is the lesson you have taught us. We start our journey far richer having known you, and if there are any like us who still live, we must share our lesson with them. We will always be by your side, as you will be with us. No distance, no sea, no danger can ever stand between us. You, dear Prince, have become our brother. No longer the Brother's Three, we shall be known, as the Brother's Four. When asked who you are, we will have the same answer—he is a brave, generous, and wise man, noble born who we are proud to call brother."

Knowing that it must be this way did little to ease the ache in the Prince's heart. One does not often make such good friends. Yet, friendship also meant letting friends go to seek their own happiness. Knowing this did not make the loss any easier. Turning to his friends, one by one, the Prince finally spoke, "Brothers, I shall say that I have three brothers, brave and true, who wander the world helping those in need. Selfless and brave, all those they call friend, are also my friend."

Watching his brothers smile, all the Prince could say was, "I wish that you could stay near my side, for your friendship and consul could not mean more to me than if we were born brothers."

Silently watching the fire, seated in a circle as was their custom, the silence was broken by Duncan. "No one said we would never see each other again."

This was followed by Otis saying, "We'll be back to see you—often."

Then Brewster added his voice, "We will return to make sure that you have indeed named your children Brewster, Duncan, and Otis, if the Princess will allow it."

Smiling, the Prince replied, "Knowing what kind heart lies within the Princess, have no doubt. Brewster, Duncan, and Otis it shall be."

Little sleeping took place that evening, as they talked and talked through the night. Now, in the safety of a warm fire and secure in the knowledge that they had succeeded in all that they had done, it was a time to remember the little joys of their journey. Duncan trying to thread a needle, Otis's restless nights that left trees uprooted each morning, and most of all how their deeds had freed a Queen. No matter how many stories were told, there was always one more to tell. Finally, knowing that their adventures together were enough to fill a lifetime of stories, they sat quietly enjoying what they knew was to be their last night together, or at least until they met again.

The following morning found all four friends waking at the same moment, at the first rays of sunshine. It was as if all lay motionless waiting for the first reason to rise from their silent waiting, because all knew that once they awoke they would have to say their goodbyes. Little was said that morning; for all knew that it would be a long time between their goodbye and seeing each other again. The Prince could find no words to express all he wished to say, and neither could his friends. Yet, it was not longing for his friends which brought sadness; it was his desire for them to share his happiness. They had experienced much together, laughter, hardship, fear, and even great courage. Now, he longed to have them join him in great joy.

Knowing what was troubling the Prince, Brewster spoke, "We share in your great joy today, but also remember that you share in our joy. Now, you must hurry, there is a Princess and Queen, as well as many worried villagers whom await your return. Quickly, end their fear, you must return to show yourself safe from harm."

"Yes, yes I must go," said the Prince, "but before I leave, we must sit once more around the morning fire."

And so it was, the four friends sat around the morning fire, knowing that while everything was going to be different, life is always different, but, having been together, it would also be better. Once the fire had turned to little more than a fading glow in the morning sun, the Prince stood, and opened his mouth to speak, but stopped before a word was spoken. Brewster, Otis and Duncan also stood, and they, too, were unable to speak. Slapping the dust from his pants, he gave one last look and smile at his friends, and with his hair falling before his eyes, he turned and walked into the morning sun.

Although he knew that he would miss his friends, the more he walked, the more his thoughts turned from missing his friends to the unknown challenge that he knew he was soon to face. Trekking back to what he believed was to be a new and happy life with the Princess, he reflected on the moment when the Princess handed him the thread from her tapestry. She had whispered, "This thread links my past to the future, for it is the same thread that my family has used to weave the tapestry which holds the names of all my ancestors. It shall be the thread that reveals my wedding for future generations. My future is now in your hands."

While he walked, under a clear blue sky, further from his friends and closer to the Princess, he slowly fingered the silken thread nestled within the tiny satchel. Each step, not only brought him closer to the Princess, but also to a deeper understanding of what was to happen, what needed to happen. Now, as if his eyes were no longer clouded, he did not need to see the tiny holes, for he now understood their meaning. He knew he was being watched, and he knew that he would see the tiny holes if he looked. Sensing that the one who had been shadowing his every step was near, he began walking more and more slowly, as if he were tiring from the long walk. Slower and slower he walked, more and more wearily, until he finally stopped amidst some thick bushes.

Wishing to keep himself well hidden, and not seen by whom he knew watched, he laid down atop a large flat rock hidden on three sides. After several minutes of not moving, as if asleep, he slowly removed first the necklace, and then the silken thread from his secret pocket. Knowing what needed to be done, he worked swiftly and silently—confident, that from a distance, it would appear as if he were napping.

Once he returned the necklace to his pocket, he slowly stirred, as if truly awaking from a nap. Gathering his belongings, he resumed his journey prepared and ready, but still unsure of what was to happen. Although the Prince had not walked any great distance, he knew he was being followed. Yet, when he secretly turned and glanced backwards to check his progress, he never saw anyone, only the ever-present holes, which crisscrossed his own footsteps. Putting aside his eagerness to return to the Princess, he knew that it would be best to slowly shift his path away from the Princess, knowing that if evil followed, he did not want to bring it to the castle gate.

Walking and waiting, his mind turned to the good people of his own village and his three dear friends. The more he walked, the more he thought of them, and the more they brought both comfort and strength for what lay ahead. Thinking about his life before he began this quest, he realized how much he had changed, how much he had learned, and most of all how much he looked at life differently. Just as his thoughts were shifting from the villagers and friends so dear to his heart, to the Princess who also dwelled in his heart, he knew he was not alone. He did not have to look, for he knew that this time, he need not turn his head quickly to find the one who had been following.

Chapter Ten

Slowly turning, the Prince spoke, "I see that you finally now have the courage to make yourself known to me." Noticing the startled look upon this stranger mere steps away, the Prince waited for an answer.

"Why, young man, do you address me like that, I have been struggling to catch up with you, but it is difficult for an old man, such as myself, to keep pace with a young one."

Recognizing that his soft words masked a dark heart, but not wishing to reveal all that he knew, the Prince replied, "I must have mistaken you for someone else, for during my trip, accompanied by friends, someone followed, but did not reveal himself. I thought maybe you were afraid of my friends."

"No, I may be old, but I fear no one, not two, or even three...." It was a tiny slip, but the Prince now knew for certain, it was this man who had followed him. Who else would know that his friends numbered three?

Acting as if the Stranger's slip had gone unnoticed, the Prince in a friendly tone continued,

"Are you familiar with this forest, for I appear to be lost and am unable to find my way to the village I seek."

"No," replied the stranger. "This forest is not well known to me, but I have heard that a small village lies not too distant from here. Maybe we can walk together for a while."

The Prince knew that the stranger's words dripped evil, but not wishing to reveal his plan, merely answered, "Yes, maybe that would be enjoyable."

Off they walked, in the direction that the stranger said would bring them to the castle. "Tell me young man, why do you seek this castle?"

"I am to marry a beautiful and kind Princess, born of a noble father and mother."

After a moments silence, the stranger relied, "Ahhh, so your betrothed waits eagerly for you. Well, I wish you nothing but happiness. Yet, your clothes are worn, your shoes nearly broken, you don't appear to make a very good husband. You must be carrying precious gifts to win over her heart. That must be the case; what gifts do you bring her?"

The Prince looked closely at the stranger, and then, in the words of a simple man, spoke yet again, "None, sir, only the love that I carry in my heart."

"But, that cannot be true. Is it not true that she will only marry the bridegroom who brings her dead father's necklace as a gift?" asked the stranger.

Knowing that the stranger had revealed his true intent, the Prince continued, "Yes, that is true, I possess that necklace."

Now, with his voice struggling to mask his rising anger, the stranger continued, "But, but, you said that you carried no gift, what man would lie to an old man such as myself? First you say that you bring no gift and then you tell me that you carry a necklace for her favor."

The Prince looked carefully at the stranger and judging him for what he truly was, finally spoke, "I carry no gift for her from me. I carry the gift her father had set aside for her. It is his gift, not mine. But, did you not say that you did not know this land, yet you know of this challenge and that her father the king is dead? Now, tell me friend, what stranger would lie to a young man?"

Not waiting for a reply from the stranger, for the stranger had no words to offer, knowing that his deception was lost, the Prince continued, "Would you like to see it? Would you like to see what you have searched for all these years? Has your memory so faded that you need to see it once more? Has not it brought enough misery to the world to please your dark heart?"

Even as the Prince's words left his mouth, he knew that they would mean nothing to the stranger. He was past understanding. He was lost. Still, he waited for a reply, hoping that his words had reached somewhere he could not see.

He was to be disappointed, for as soon as his hope rose because of the stranger's silence, it was dashed once again, as the stranger began to speak with his words sputtering with hate, "No, no it has not. You think yourself wise, but you are foolish to challenge me. Know this, I shall possess it this very day. I have not spent a lifetime seeking it only to have you return it to a Princess who should have died years ago. It shall be mine, mine forever."

Keeping close his plan, and ready to accept this new challenge, the Prince softly and calmly spoke as if a whisper, "No, it will not. This necklace shall be returned to the Princess for whom it was made. Nothing shall prevent this necklace from caressing the neck of a father's daughter."

"You speak bravely for a young man. Do you not know that many have died trying to keep that necklace from me? Do you wish to be the next?"

"So be it. I may be next, but you shall never possess this necklace, you have sent many into the deep sea, only to find death as you forced them to get it for you, too much the coward to retrieve it yourself. No, the Princess may have to wait longer to wear it, she may even never wear it, but know this—YOU will NEVER possess it—that is the promise I make to you."

Snickering at such talk, the Stranger slowly walked around the Prince, and as he did so, he plunged the tip of his walking stick into the soft earth leaving behind a circle of small holes with every step.

The Prince watched as he did so, and when the stranger had almost completely circled him, spoke, "Do you think, I did not notice the holes that your staff made as you cowardly followed me, afraid to show yourself when my companions were by my side."

The Quest

Growing angrier and angrier, the stranger hastened his walking, until he had completely surrounded the Prince.

Once more, the Prince spoke, "I do not fear you, and I will not run when the earth opens beneath my feet."

In a rage, with the words spitting from his mouth, the stranger roared, "We shall see, you will beg me to take the necklace." Then, raising his staff above his head, his eyes turning first yellow and then red, muttered in a language the Prince could not understand. As his words fell flat among all that was dead, the earth began to rumble and the tiny holes pulled apart—until the Prince was surrounded by a circle of holes. Even in the early sunlight, the Prince could not see their bottom.

"Tell me, Prince, do you fear that I may cast you into these holes upon the earth? Do you fear them like all those that feared the bottom of the sea as I cast them down for failing to retrieve the necklace for me?"

"No. For if I am cast into these holes, it will be me that guards the Princess's necklace. I would prefer death knowing that I protect the Princess than life knowing that she would never be safe from you once you possess this necklace. Do not think me foolish, I know that you have only allowed the Queen and Princess to live because you believed that some day someone would seek it for them, and then you would easily steal it before it was returned to the true owner. It was only your greed for the necklace that halted your hatred and your desire to kill the Queen and the Princess. It was your greed that has kept them safe all these years. Once you possess the necklace, you will bring harm to those I have come to love. Your cold dead hands will never know the soft warmth of these pearls. Cast me into their depths, if you wish, but I will carry the necklace to my death."

Now, thinking that he had the better of the Prince, the stranger spoke coldly, "Do you not think that I could open these holes, once again, after your death? All I need do is raise my walking stick, and I can make any one of these holes fill and then reopen." When his words had fled his mouth, he lifted his walking stick, and the hole that he had selected, filled and then opened once again.

Beaming with evil pride, he turned to the Prince, but before he could speak, the Prince spoke almost quietly and with the hint of a smile that said the Prince would never fear this evil man. "Then tell me stranger, why did you not split the sea so as to walk upon dry land between the towering mountains of water to retrieve the necklace?"

Already knowing the answer, the Prince stared at the stranger, only to watch him sputter his words, "I can only undo that which I have done. I did not create the sea." Then, as if to prove some power over nature, he boasted, "I may not be able to split the sea in two, but I am able to move about as I wish, I have the power to block out the stars, should I so desire."

With those words, the Prince learned what he feared the most to hear, it was this evil stranger that caused the death of his father. It was true; he was the evil that caused the stars to blink that long evening of his father's death. Controlling his body, and not letting the hurt that first flashed, and then left waves of pain throughout his being confuse him, spoke, "You have killed many noble men in your life, have you not?"

"I have killed no one; they have chosen to die when they have not done my bidding. They have given their lives up for some misguided nobility. They would rather die at the tap of my walking stick, then to honor me with their loyalty. But, tell me young Prince, you do not wish death, do you?"

The Prince studied the evil stranger that stood before him, knowing that he had been the cause of his father's death, that his father had sacrificed his own life to spare his villagers from evil. The Prince also knew that while he was prepared to follow his father, that would do little to protect the Princess and the Queen. Should he die this day and the Stranger hold the necklace in his evil hands, the Princess and Queen were sure to follow him to his own death. There was still hope; the Prince had planned well, for he knew in his heart that he was to meet the evil that had been the cause of all this sorrow.

Stepping back, the Prince looked beyond the circle of holes with no bottom, to where the Stranger was standing. Without saying a word, he reached up into his sleeve and let the necklace slip into his hand, holding it in his hand; he looked closely at its beauty, and longed for the day when he could see it resting upon the neck of the Princess he loved. Then, holding it up for the Stranger to see, he asked, "Is this the cause of your greed? Is this the object that you have surrendered your life to hold? Is this what you have buried your life to steal?"

Chapter Eleven

There was to be no reply, all the Prince could see was that the Stranger was now staring at the necklace he held in his hand, and as he watched, the more he noticed that the stranger began to look less and less a man, until no longer a man—he was just evil. Sensing the right moment, the Prince held it even closer to the stranger and spoke, "Is this what you seek, is this what you have killed to possess? Take it then, take it!" Even before the last word had left his mouth, the Prince took one last hopeful look at the necklace, and then pretending to hand it to the stranger, let it drop into the largest of the holes that surrounded him prisoner.

An evil sound filled the air as the stranger looked first at the falling necklace and then the Prince, dripping anger in his voice the stranger spoke, "It is mine now, and then you shall die knowing that the Princess and the Queen will soon follow you and your father the King." Once his words died without the faintest echo, the stranger cast himself into the hole. Without a moment of doubt or hesitation, the Prince also dove into the hole, following the stranger. The stranger, with only the necklace consuming his thoughts, did not notice the Prince also falling behind him. Seeing the necklace only inches from his shrunken evil hands, he let go his walking stick to grab at the necklace, which fell just out of reach.

As his fingers were clawing their way closer and closer to the necklace, the Prince falling close behind was reaching for the walking stick, hoping that he would be able to grasp it before the stranger's fingers encircled the necklace. First one finger, then a second, and finally he had it in his grasp. Working quickly, with his right hand firmly grasped around the stick, he spun it sideways, jamming it into the walls of the hole. Jarred to a halting stop, he watched as the stranger continued to fall, his hands crawling first at what he would never possess, the necklace, and then the sides of the wall, hoping to stop his fall.

As the Prince watched the evil stranger descend into the deep darkness, the sun now moved directly overhead, its light filling the top of the once darkened hole. Lit brightly with the noonday sunlight, the Prince no longer looked at the stranger, although he could still hear his screams. What filled his eyes was the golden glimmer of the thread that the Princess had given him. It no longer just linked the past to the future. Now, stretched tight and radiating in the bright light of day, it now joined his wrist to the necklace, which dangled and sparkled in the dazzling sunlight.

Spinning in the blazing sunlight at the end of the glowing thread, he now saw the necklace in a different light. No longer was it merely a beautiful necklace. No longer was it just a loving gift from a father to a daughter. It was a link between the present and the future. It held all the dreams that a father had for his daughter, it was all about hope, and although this father would not be present to place his gift upon his daughter's neck the day she married, his hope, his love, and his wish was to come true. All that had happened was to fulfill that dream for a better place, a better time, a better life.

The Princess's father knew it when he crafted it, and his father knew it the day that he traded his life for those of the villagers and his family, it was all about sacrificing the moment in hope for a better future. Now, with the help of his village family, three dear friends, and the Princess's trust to give him her family's tapestry tread without knowing for sure if he would return, he now knew what they had always known.

Once the new path of his life was clear to him in the brilliant sunshine, his mind turned to what to do next. The Prince now found himself, hanging onto a walking stick wedged between the walls of a bottomless pit by one arm, as a priceless gift tied to his other arm spun beneath him by a thread. Knowing what to do next, he slowly wound the thread around his fingers, with the necklace drawing closer to his grasp with each turn. Once he had it safely in his hand, he put the necklace to his mouth and using his teeth bit through the glimmering thread. Now free from the thread, he immediately decided upon what to do next. Looking up, and then studying which way was free of the other holes, and with hope in his heart and his aim, he tossed the necklace out of the hole. Without peering into his heart, such an action might be foolish, but in his heart, it was what he needed to do. The Prince knew that climbing out of the hole was to be dangerous; he might fall, and be buried deep within the earth. Now, at least he could keep tight his hope, that once freed, there was a chance, even if it was only the tiniest of chances that the necklace might still find its way to the Princess.

Free from worry about the safety of the necklace, he began his climb. At first, it was slow and difficult; only by squeezing himself between the walls was he able to slowing wedge his way closer to freedom. As difficult as the climb was, the Prince held on to his hope as much as he held tight the walls of the bottomless pit, for as he clamored nearer and nearer to the land above; he noticed that the roots of trees, long dead, were slowly filling the once empty hole. Grabbing onto the roots, the climb became easier and easier, until he reached the good earth above.

Collapsing upon the cool earth, he thought what next to do. In his hand he still held the walking stick, which had saved his life but caused so much sorrow for others. He did not have to think for very long. Standing up, he took both ends of the stick in his hands, and striking it upon his knee, broke it in two. Looking at the two broken pieces that he held in his hands, he did not notice what had happened immediately upon the loud snap of breaking wood. The holes were gone. With the disappearance of the holes, the Prince knew that never again would the Princess and Queen need to fear the evil stranger who now lied buried deep within the earth.

Taking the necklace in his hands, he examined it closely to find the place where he had tied the thread. He almost missed finding it, since it was so tiny, having been cut near the strand of silk that bound the pearls together. As he was about to remove it, he thought better of it, and leaving it where he had first tied it, he carefully placed the necklace within the same small satchel that the Princess had given him, and which had held the thread that saved his life. Then, carefully untying the thread from his wrist, wishing to waste none of it, he placed it along with the necklace into the tiny satchel.

Once the necklace was safely tucked away, cushioned by the thread that was also there, he slipped it back into his secret pocket, which lied, near his heart. He then sought out the roots, which having saved his life, now lay upon the ground. Taking up the softest he could find, he used them to tie the two broken pieces of the walking stick together, and placed them out of sight, for he no longer wished to see them.

Once these tasks were completed, he sat down, and let his mind and heart wander to all that had happened during the past several weeks. Even amidst all the danger, he thought himself fortunate. Even the death of his father, long a mystery to him, could now be understood. His father had traded his life for the safety of his village. He could only hope that at the moment of his father's sacrifice, he held tight the hope that someday, someone would finally bring an end to the evil, which threatened his village. His father's sacrifice had meaning, his death meaning. He was but one step in the path to end this evil. It may have taken many years, but now evil was gone.

Sitting beneath a large tree, one that moments before had not stood, he rested silently under its cooling shade, reading and rereading the note that the Princess had floated to his waiting hands. It was only after reading it many times, that he began to carefully fold it as the Princess had done moments before she watched it sail to the Prince's waiting hands. As he did so, he noticed how soft the creases had become from the many times that he had sought its comfort during his quest.

Holding it in his hands he remembered what Otis had told him. Some words, some thoughts can only be known to those who speak or write them and the one who listens or reads them. Gently sliding the note back to his secret pocket, and then checking twice to make sure it was safe, his thoughts turned to what the future might bring. Gazing quietly upon the meadow that surrounded him, which hours before had been a vast scorching desert, his mood, along with the earth had changed.

No longer thinking of the evil that had once existed, he began to think about his friends, and all they had taught him. He thought about the Princess, whose simple gesture of entrusting him with the thread that her family held dear, had saved his live. He thought about his village, and how he wished he could find a way to let them know that he had found happiness, but the more he thought about it, the more he began to realize that they might already

The Quest

know.

Sitting alone, but not lonely, for his friends were with him, he realized that he had started his journey as a young Prince, but had grown into a man. He wished, in his heart that his parents could be with him, to tell him that it was their love that allowed him to win the day. Yet, while this was not to be, his hope was strong enough to know that they too shared in his joy.

Now well rested, he knew that there was still much to be done. He needed to return to the Queen and Princess—only then could his journey come to an end. Rising from his needed rest, he collected his belongings, checked the secret pocket that held a father's gift, and set himself upon the task of walking. Although he had made this same walk many times, never before had he beheld the great beauty that lied before his eyes. Brewster was right, sometimes one does not see what is right there before us. No longer a young man, he could now see what a man could see. Walking and thinking, the walk was quickly over, even before the Prince knew that he had arrived. Deep in thought, the Prince did not even notice the awe-struck villagers silently watching him as he drew nearer and nearer to the castle.

Crossing the many fields and orchards that surrounded the castle, he entered through the main gate, but not before trying once again to ring the bell which made no sound. Knowing that there was one more task, which still needed to be done, he entered the gate to find everyone frozen in place as he walked into the castle.

Chapter Twelve

Carrying the tiny red satchel trimmed with gold that the Princess had given him, the guards stared spellbound at the sight, wondering if this tiny purse held the pearl necklace that everyone thought impossible to recover. When he reached the room where the Queen was waiting for him, he approached the Queen and bowed before her. The Queen said not a word, but as the Prince began to offer the small satchel to the her, terror crossed over her face as she caught a glimpse of the shimmering pearls. The Guard Captain, sensing the Queen's fear, quickly stepped between the Prince and the Queen, blocking his way.

Leaning off to one side, to see the Queen behind the Captain, the Prince quietly spoke, "There is no longer a reason to fear this necklace. The ocean tides have long ago washed clean the poison placed upon it, but, no ocean tide could wash away the love your beloved husband and King had for his daughter the Princess. No longer need you fear the man behind this evil, for he too has been defeated. He is dead. Not by the hand of someone more evil than he, but consumed by his own evil and greed.

He died as he lived, seeking to steal the necklace first from the King and then from the hands that labored for its return. Now, his bones lay buried deep beneath the sand in a grave dug by his own evil hands. No longer can he hurt the Princess. She is free, as is her mother."

The words spoken by the Prince worked as if they were a salve that finally soothed an old wound that although healed, still bore a painful scar. As the pain floated away from her face, the hardness seen in her eyes also began to melt away, replaced with a look of kindness and understanding. The Prince, seeing the change occur, once again spoke. "During my quest, I have learned much, I have learned that your beloved King was murdered by an evil man seeking to own this necklace. Realizing that the King would never part with his daughter's gift while she lived, he tried to poison the Princess by placing an evil potion on the necklace, thinking that once she was dead, the King would not be able to bear to see it again and would sell it to him to be rid of it. Little could this evil man have known that the King would place a kiss upon the necklace out of love for his daughter, and the poison would quickly work its evil only to make a village mourn the passing of its King. You were wise, dear Queen, to cast it to the bottom of the ocean when he later threatened the Princess upon your refusal to sell him the necklace. There, lying at the bottom of the sea, where the pearls were first born, the poison has been washed away, washed away by the many tears its evil has caused. They have been reborn—they are now what they always were—a gift from a loving father to his daughter to wear on her wedding day."

Nothing else needed to be said, and as the Queen quietly sat, the Prince handed the satchel that safeguarded the necklace to the Guard Captain to give to the Queen. After removing it from the purse, he carefully examined the necklace, and satisfied that it was indeed safe, he turned to give it to the Queen. Looking at the necklace and the Guard Captain before her, it was no longer a look of fear that traced itself across the Queen's face. Rather, it was the look of someone gazing upon an object that brings back memories of someone loved dearly, long ago. After several moments, with no one speaking or moving, the Queen looked up until her misty eyes met those of the Guard Captain. "Dear friend, hold tight the necklace, while I speak with the Prince."

Settling back into her chair, the Queen sat quietly peering into the eyes of the young man who stood before her, wondering how, even with help, he could have answered the challenges she had placed before him. She did not have to decide whether she liked him or not. She knew that she had found a fondness in her heart for him the moment he had stood before her. Neither bold nor brash, yet confident and comfortable with himself, he reminded her of her husband.

Standing on the uppermost balcony of the castle, hidden behind a large column and unseen by the young couple, she had seen the Prince and Princess together when they first met. A vision that reminded the Queen of when she first met her husband. Now, a generation later, this young Prince stood at the bottom of the stairs holding flowers that bloomed only once every tenth Spring, and looked very much like her husband when they had first met. Looking at the young couple from afar, she knew that her daughter looked at the Prince as she had looked at the King. The deeper she looked into the heart of the Prince, the more she knew that he had done more than just answer three challenges, he had freed her daughter and in doing so had also freed her.

Images and old memories flooded her mind, overwhelming every other thought. Images of her husband and the happiness that was their brief life together. Memories, which long hidden, now blazed as vibrant as when she had first hid them in her heart. They had not dimmed even in all the years they were hidden away. How could this be? But she knew that it was because of the Prince. He had carried them across the bridge from darkness into the sunlight, where they were free to be shared. No longer locked away and guarded, she knew that she would never allow it to fade again.

With new found happiness and joy, and knowing the warmth of the heart which lived within the Prince, the Queen extended her hand to him and spoke, "There is more to tell, I sense that you also have been touched by this evil, now tell me why?"

The Prince replied, "Yes, dear Queen, my life has been touched by this evil too. It has been the cause of my dear father's death, and while this knowledge brings understanding and merit to his death, it also brings sadness."

The Queen, knowing the pain that such sadness brings to a young heart, could only offer, "The loss you feel today is a loss that you will always feel. But know this, I speak to you as a mother to a son. Rest your thoughts my son, your parents rejoice in the happiness you have won this day, find comfort in the joy you have brought to them.

Quiet reigned over the village, as everyone let the meaning of what had happened that day settle into their hearts and minds. Finally, rousing everyone from their quiet, came the sound of a young boy shouting, "Well, are they going to get married?"

The Queen turned to the young boy whom she knew quite well, and answered, "It is up to the Prince and Princess, but what do you think?"

Thinking a moment, the young man, now nearly hanging over the castle's wall replied, "If they love each other, why not?"

Now it was the Queen's turn to speak, but no words were needed, for as the Queen turned to look upon the Prince and Princess, they also turned and each spoke, "Yes, we do love each other, very much."

The Queen turned back to the young man, high above the courtyard, and said, "Well, young man, it is okay with me, how about you? What do you say, should they marry?"

"Yup" was all that was heard, and that was enough for everyone, the Prince, Princess, Queen, and the entire village.

Amidst the celebration and rejoicing, the

Prince, pulling tight the Princess to his side, whispered in her ear. "When you gaze upon the necklace, notice the tiny bit of thread that lies nestled between the loveliest of pearls. Please leave it there tied, and each time you look upon it, know in your heart that it was your kindness that saved my life."

The Princess looked into the Prince's eyes, first quizzically, and then lovingly with the slightest of nods, one of the tiny gestures that speak more than words among two people in love.

Once the celebrating and cheering had settled down to where people could once again speak, the Guard Captain, as if it was the only thing left to do, approached the Queen with the necklace that now laid upon the satchel which had safeguarded not only the necklace and thread, but had held the key to the Prince's success. The Queen seeing him approach spoke so that all present could hear.

"My dear protector, Captain of the Guard, and dear friend of my beloved husband the King, hold tight that necklace, for it shall be you who places it upon the neck of the Princess. Throughout these past many years, years in which I was too bitter and fearful to bring joy into my daughter's life, you not only protected the Princess from harm, you were her haven, you were her friend. Looking back, you could not have loved her more if she had been your own daughter. You have not only loved her as a daughter, she has looked to you as only a daughter would look upon a father. As the King lay dying and after asking you to watch over his family, he turned to me and told me to trust you in all matters since you were a kind and noble man, a man who could be trusted with our lives. Now, I too, have come to realize that my husband's faith in you was true. No King, no man, could have had a more faithful friend, and I know in my heart, that his memory would be honored, if you would not only place the necklace upon her neck, but also accompany her as she walks to her marriage vows."

Once the Queen stopped speaking, the Princess made her way to the Captain, no longer able to run beneath his legs, she stood beside him and placed her arms around his waist. After many seconds had passed without a word between them, the Princess spoke, "Captain, you would honor me by walking me to my wedding," then whispering ever so quietly into the Captain's ears, "and I promise not to hide beneath your coat."

The Captain, now wearing a smile broad enough to match his broad shoulders, knelt, and lovingly whispered, "The honor and privilege will be mine. But first, I have many stories about your father that I have not shared with you before, which you should hear before you wed. Shall we go sit upon our special step?"

After smiling, and a slight nod, the Princess took the Captain's hand, approached her mother and kissing her on the cheek thanked her for her blessing. Reaching out, the Queen touched the Princess's cheek, and thanked her for the many blessings that she, as a faithful and loving daughter, had bestowed upon her.

After one more embrace, the Princess turned

back to the Prince and spoke, "Dear Prince, I look forward to our future together, but now I must speak with the Captain, who has been a father to me and who I know will treat you like a son also."

Smiling, the Prince bowed, and in a loving tone, addressed the Queen's daughter, "Princess, I await the rest of my life with you, but go now and be with the Guard Captain. As for me, there still remains one more task to ensure our life and safety together. I leave you now, but you will never leave my heart."

Leaving the castle, the Prince walked back to where he had defeated evil, and then seeking out the highest hill, he climbed to the top, and laid upon the hill's peak staring into the night sky. It was not long before he was thinking of his mother and father, and how he longed for them to be there, he thought about his home village and its kind villagers. He also thought about his three brothers and all they had done for him, but most of all he thought about all that they had taught him. Thinking about his brothers, it was not long before he began to look upon the stars, the same stars that he gazed upon each night with his friends as they laid beside the fire telling each other stories about their lives. However, tonight the stars looked different, and he knew that now was the time to complete the final task, which still remained.

Gathering up twigs and brushwood for kindling, he arranged all that he had gathered into three mounds. Striking his fire flint, he set ablaze the first bundle of wood. Moving on to second bundle, and then the third, it was not long before all three bonfires were blazing. Slowly walking to where he had hidden it, he removed the two-halves of what was left of the walking stick, and tossed them into the largest of the three fires. As he did so, the fire roared bright and exploded in a large puff of smoke, which sailed forth from the earth circling in the air, spinning closer and closer to the village, which stood off in the distance. Edging nearer and nearer, it began to encircle the spires of the castle and village. Without really knowing why he knew, the Prince knew what was to happen. Twisting and turning its way through the village, bells could be heard peeling in the distance. No longer was sorrow to dwell in the village, for with the burning of the walking stick, evil had been vanquished. Now it was joy that rang the once silent bells. The curse was gone—and gone forever.

Having done what needed to be done, the Prince sat among the blazing fires thinking about his friends, who far away, further than a man running could travel in four days, sat around their own blazing fire. Where, like those that they had many times surrounded with their friend the Prince, they talked until the fire had turned to glowing embers and its light cast a warm golden glow. They talked about their adventure, as well as their journeys alone and together, each waiting for some sign of their friend's wedding. Throughout the evening, Duncan and Otis strained to be alert to any sign they might hear or see. Only Brewster seemed at ease.

As the morning's sapphire glow began to brighten the sky, Brewster looked upwards to see the still visible shape of the two falcons. Although Brewster knew their shape well, and where to find them regardless of the season, this time they snuggled closer than he had ever seen them before. Gazing intently, a smile formed upon his lips just moments before he heard Otis and Duncan hurriedly rising and staring into the horizon.

In all the excitement, Otis and Duncan did not notice Brewster's brightening smile because they were straining to hear what only Otis could hear and only Duncan could see. It was not too long before Otis announced, "I hear three bells pealing from the village."

Duncan proclaimed, "And I see three fires blazing."

Brewster, although unable to either hear the chiming bells or see the flames blazing, knew well before his brothers that their friend had found happiness. Brewster did not have to hear faraway bells or see flickering flames, he knew from the warmth of his heart, that his friend the Prince was also staring into the heavens, and this time, he too, could see the two falcons.

ACKNOWLEDGMENTS

The effort required to write this book would have been impossible without the help and support of many friends and family, only a few of whom are mentioned here.

Ryan and Rebecca, who have taught me about nobility every day of their lives; Meghan Reilly, who sitting beside me one very early Saturday morning while Ryan played ice hockey, listened wide-eyed and attentive; Breana Beaudreault, whose enthusiasm and excitement confirmed for me that the story was worth retelling, and Catherine Reidy, although only eight years old, provided me with insight well beyond her years.

Marc Thibodeau, who diligently persevered the editing of every sentence and phrase; Jamie Ennis, who recognized early in the story's writing, that benefiting from the trials of others without risk to oneself is never noble. Lyn Stanzione, who patiently guided me through the final editing, layout, cover design and offered the encouragement to both finish and publish the story.

Finally, Lyn Ucci, who reintroduced me to the wonder and importance of children's literature during my college years. Remembering her, sitting beside me on a dorm floor, and reading aloud, "They roared their terrible roars and gnashed their terrible teeth…" has always remained one of the magical moments of my life.

AFTERWARD

The retelling of this story owns as much of its existence to my father's inability to see anything go to waste—as it does to my own efforts. Looking back, the birth of this retold fable took place on an average morning in 1959, while I was being deposited at our local school for yet another day of kindergarten.

Somewhere, while being accompanied between the front seat of a 1960 Plymouth Belvedere and my kindergarten classroom, my father spotted a book lying atop some far less interesting trash in one of the several wastepaper baskets, which lined the classroom corridor at regular intervals. While the graceful slight of hand needed to side step to the wastebasket, pick it up, and ultimately purloin the manuscript is well remembered—I can offer no potential witnesses to collaborate my side of the story—which reflects the stealth in which it was accomplished. Even with the brief glance afforded me, the transaction was impressive—first it was there, and then it wasn't. Although impressed with my father's quick hand, and rescue from what would have assuredly been a burial at the city dump, I gave it no more thought. However, later that same day, sometime after the end of dinner, the book reappeared in my father's hand and then thrust into my possession with the pronouncement—You should read this! Unsure whether a gift or a challenge—my greedy hands snatched possession of the pinched manuscript.

I descended the always-counted 13 stairs that led to my castle refuge, the unfinished portion of an otherwise finished basement. Checking to ensure that I had not been followed, I ducked into my cubby. It was bordered on one side by the chimney, on another by a retrofitted oil furnace that had been built to be fueled by coal—all of which was encircled by the backsides of the newly installed knotty-pine boards. Secure within my furnace fortress, I set myself to examining the tattered bounty which my hands now held.

Even a quick look confirmed its abused state—the original front cover, table of contents, and several of the opening stories had been stripped away. What was left of the book was held together by what remained of the barely attached back-cover and the exposed spine of flaked glue and frayed treads. Lacking a cover, along with the first 50 or so pages—the easy read pages—I knew that it had little intrinsic value. Had the remnants been worth even a mere nickel, it would have joined the scores of books that went from library shelves to the annual book sale. Moreover, residing in a home where the number of books was calculated by the linear foot, I knew of books far more valuable than this book with its frayed pages and earthy smell that I now turned over and over in my hands. Yet, this book was special—exquisitely special—for it was unique among all the books which lined the walls and competed for our living space. Valuable, not because of the colorful and whimsical pictures which appeared every few pages, and not because many of the words were yet undecipherable to me. No, this book, which I now held in my hands had been stolen by my father—there could be no doubt that the Sisters of Mercy had already discovered that a thief had occurred during their trash review prior to placement on the curb for pickup.

While "owner abandonment" may have even trumped "removing without permission" in a court of law, Catholic school was not a world governed by the nuances of law and a plaintiff's pleading. Catholic schools in the early 60's had well defined and illuminated lines, usually with blinking neon lights, which clearly separated what was sinful and what was not. Worse, whereas one might hope for God's understanding and forgiveness for the well-intentioned transgressor, forgiveness and mercy from the Good Sisters was somewhat less abundant.

Yet, regardless of what the "taking" was called or my father's state of mind—I now held the very first book I ever owned. Even the missing 50 or so pages was of no consequence, since typical of all primers, those beginning first pages—were little more than "baby stories." The real stories, the "novels" rich with giants and magical beings, resided towards the end of the book. Here the stories were both lengthy and complex—the short ones may have only been 200 words or so long, but the longer ones might be all of 400 words and contained words I had never seen before—many of which defied even my best efforts.

Among the many tattered tales that did remain, this story was my favorite—which even my father, having read it hundreds of times, was known to attest. The story retold here, whose actual title is long forgotten and defies all efforts to remember, was sandwiched between "The Sun and the North Wind" and a story about a Brownie. Most, if not all the stories included within what was left of the book, were known to me in one form or another. One story, the story retold here, was completely unknown to me. Yet, all these years later, this one story remains as vivid to me as it did the first time I labored to sound out the unknown words it contained.

While the story's original title is long forgotten, or possibly never known due to the book's tattered condition, I never forgot the story. Locked away in my memory, it could be readily recalled on those rare occasions when I was entrusted with the care of a young child. Although unsure whether the calming results of the telling were due to the story's interest or my mere recitation—the retelling kept the story alive. As the years passed, each retelling became longer, some characters were expanded, new characters were added, and in one case a character was eliminated—the ever-present and quintessential fairytale character—the evil stepmother.

Over the years that passed, multiple efforts were made to locate the original and tattered primer—without success. Scores of librarians, children's literature professors, and peers were asked if they remembered the story—no one did, not even a faint remembrance. New and used bookstores were rifled, thrift stores explored, and the children's section of libraries were explored without luck.

Yet, all was not despair—since out of that failure, you now hold the retelling of that story.

ABOUT THE AUTHOR

Robert S Bucci lives in Providence, Rhode Island and has two adult children, his son Ryan Stephen, and daughter Rebecca Ann.

RsB is the director of the Research Analytics Unit for the Center for Health Care Financing at the University of Massachusetts Medical School. Prior to his work at UMASS Medical School, he was Research Director of the UMASS Poll at the McCormack Center at the University's Boston Campus. Bucci received his MSPA from the University of Massachusetts John W. McCormack Graduate School of Public Affairs, and is a graduate of Rhode Island College and LaSalle Academy in Providence.

Most nights, RsB can be found stargazing in his SkyFort observatory, which sits atop his garage in Providence.

You can contact him at bucci.robert@yahoo.com

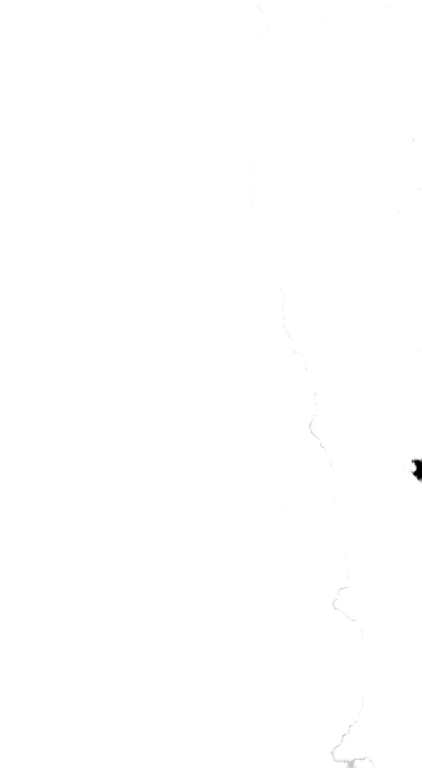

Proof

HAGIOGRAPHY

Made in the USA
Charleston, SC
27 October 2014